Miguel had taken less than two steps into the beach house before the provocative scent that was uniquely Allegra's teased his senses. His angry gaze scanned the *sala* and found her sitting on the sofa, head bowed.

This time seeing her wasn't a trick of his imagination. This time the fragrance and the woman were real.

This time retribution was in his grasp.

Though he'd known she was finally coming back, his heart gave a sharp, painful kick that was at odds with his fury. She'd broken through his defenses and made him care. She'd won his trust and his heart and then made him regret it—in the worst possible way....

For as long as **JANETTE KENNY** can remember, plots and characters have taken up residence in her head. Her parents, both voracious readers, read her the classics when she was a child. That gave birth to a deep love for literature, and allowed her to travel to exotic locales—those found between the covers of books.

Janette's artist mother encouraged her yen to write. As an adolescent she began creating cartoons featuring her dad as the hero, with plots that focused on the misadventures on their family farm, and she stuffed them in the nightly newspaper for him to find.

Her first real writing began with fan fiction, taking favorite TV shows and writing episodes and endings she loved—happily ever after, of course. In her junior year of high school, she told her literature teacher she intended to write for a living one day. His advice? Pursue the dream, but don't quit the day job.

Though she dabbled with articles, she didn't fully embrace her dream to write novels until years later, when she was a busy cosmetologist. That was when she decided to write the type of stories she'd been reading—romances.

Once the writing bug bit, the incurable passion for creating stories consumed her. Still, it was seven more years before she saw her first historical romance published. Now that she's also writing contemporary romances for Harlequin Presents®, she finally knows that a full-time career in writing is closer to reality.

Janette shares her home with a chow-shepherd pup she rescued from the pound, who aspires to be a lap dog. She invites you to visit her Web site at www.jankenny.com. She loves to hear from readers— e-mail her at janette@jankenny.com.

PROUD REVENGE, PASSIONATE WEDLOCK

JANETTE KENNY

~ DARK NIGHTS WITH A BILLIONAIRE ~

TORONTO • NEW YORK • LONDON
AMSTERDAM • PARIS • SYDNEY • HAMBURG
STOCKHOLM • ATHENS • TOKYO • MILAN • MADRID
PRAGUE • WARSAW • BUDAPEST • AUCKLAND

Recycling programs
for this product may
not exist in your area.

ISBN-13: 978-0-373-52739-7

PROUD REVENGE, PASSIONATE WEDLOCK

First North American Publication 2009.

www.eHarlequin.com

Printed in U.S.A.

PROUD REVENGE,
PASSIONATE WEDLOCK

CHAPTER ONE

ALLEGRA got a white-knuckled grip on the knob and forced her hand to open the door on the past she'd dreaded visiting again. Until one month ago, she'd remembered nothing of the previous five months.

Much of it was still shrouded in shadow. But the memories that were clear nearly killed her.

Her precious baby was dead. The husband she'd loved beyond words hadn't inquired about her health since the accident.

It was as if she'd died that day. God knows she'd wished she had after she'd realized she was to blame for the accident.

"Miguel doesn't deserve you," her uncle had told her more times than she could recall. "Divorce him."

The thought of dissolving her marriage sickened her, but she couldn't move forward with her life if she was bound in an estranged marriage. No, she needed closure.

She had to come to grips with her daughter's death. She had to sever all ties to the life that had held such promise in Cancún. And she had to do it here where it had begun.

Allegra drew in a shaky breath and stepped into the beach house where her love with Miguel had begun. She'd steeled herself to be greeted with an onslaught of cherished and troubled memories, but she was totally unprepared to cope with this soft whispering sense that she'd just come home after a long, arduous journey.

The rightness of being here played over and over in her mind as she stood on the threshold a moment and tried to slow her racing heart. It was useless, for her nerves were tied in tight apprehensive knots.

Run, her mind screamed. Run back to England and the promise of a safe, quiet life there. Run away from the tempting vibrancy that made her feel alive for the first time in months.

Determined to face the past head-on, she walked into the *sala* as she had countless times before. The spun-gold sunlight that streamed through the bank of windows to dance over the pasta tiles seemed far too welcoming for a place that should still be deep in mourning.

She'd notified the housekeeper of her return, and that kind woman must have hurried to tidy the place. She'd even left the windows open to air the house out.

It looked as if Allegra had stepped out for a day of shopping and had just returned. If only that were true—

"Señora, where would you like me to place your luggage?" her driver asked her.

"In the upstairs bedroom facing the sea, please."

Allegra was unwilling to step foot in the master bedroom this soon. Besides sleep had been a stranger to her of late. And the memories made in that room were better left undisturbed.

As if she could ever forget Miguel.

The driver toted her bags upstairs and was back in a heartbeat, hand extended. Allegra paid him for the fare from the airport, plus a generous tip.

"Gracias, señora," he said, smiling broadly in a gracious manner she'd once taken for granted.

She'd taken so much for granted. What was it they said? You never appreciated what you had until it was gone?

The heavy ache of loss washed over her like the incoming tide, threatening to erode her moorings. The doctor's warning that she wasn't strong enough to go through with this rocked her shaky confidence.

She hated the uncertainty. Hated the black void still there in her memory.

Allegra swallowed the impulsive request that the departing driver return her to the airport. She closed and locked the door, then pressed her forehead against the cool wood until her breathing steadied. Leaving would solve nothing.

Closure. She had to shut the door on the past and walk away a new woman.

She had to find peace of mind. She could think of no better place than her beach house.

Allegra turned toward the shady *palapa* where she'd relished taking her afternoon tea and drank in the tranquil sights that she'd fallen in love with when she came here two years ago. Gentle steps led down to the expanse of white sand that would be warm underfoot.

If she closed her eyes she could see herself the day she moved into this house. She'd hurried into her bikini and dashed down to the private beach. The water was warm and clear, and the gentle breeze was a sensuous massage on her skin.

England had been a world away, and she'd promised herself she'd partake of every delight the Yucatán had to offer while she made the biggest decision of her life—should she marry the very proper English doctor that she'd dated for over one year?

She liked him. She loved him in a way. But she wasn't sure of making that final commitment.

That was when Miguel had risen out of the surf like a pagan god, his bronzed body long and lean, his smile slow and sensuous, his eyes promising her pleasures she'd barely tasted.

She shook her head and smiled at that memory. She'd been sure Miguel was a beach bum. How wrong she'd been.

Even after all that had gone wrong, she remembered well how he'd wrap his arms and legs around her, holding her so close after they made love that she believed they were one. She'd been helplessly naive. Hopelessly in love.

She'd known whatever happened here, she'd never be able to marry her doctor.

Then too soon the hot Latin lover who'd swept her off her feet on the beach and caught her up in his privileged world suddenly became too busy building an empire to spend more than stolen moments with his wife and newborn child.

She'd made excuses for him that he needed time away from a fussy infant and frazzled wife. She'd waited for her lover, her husband, her hero.

But he never came.

The sun slanted just so through the windows to catch the gilded edge of a lone picture frame on the far étagère. For a moment she couldn't breathe, couldn't think, couldn't move.

She crossed to the étagère on legs that trembled. Her hands shook as she reached for the picture, her grip too tight, her heart beating too fast. Her precious baby, her Cristobel.

She'd never wanted anything as much as she'd wanted this beautiful child conceived in love. A gift from God, Miguel had said, and she'd agreed.

Her trembling finger traced the plump cheek of the life she and Miguel created when their love was new and unencumbered. How could she have been so careless with this child?

She gathered the picture to her heart and squeezed her eyes shut, but her daughter's smile filled her mind's eye and her gurgling laugh replaced the quiet that crashed in the room like an angry sea. One racking sob escaped her, then another.

Her fault, her conscience needled her as she crossed to the

sofa with the photo digging into her flesh and tears blinding her to cruel reality. Her fault.

Miguel took less than two steps into the beach house before the provocative scent that was uniquely Allegra's teased his senses. His angry gaze scanned the *sala* and found her sitting on the sofa, head bowed.

This time seeing her wasn't a trick of his imagination. This time the fragrance and the woman were real.

This time retribution was in his grasp.

Though he'd known she was finally coming back, his heart gave a sharp, painful kick that was at odds with his fury. It had been that way from the moment he'd first met her, standing like an ethereal angel at the edge of the sea, her skin white as cream and just as soft.

She'd broken through his defenses and took command of his waking and sleeping thoughts. For the first time in his life he'd nearly lost control of his emotions but that was never to be. Instead he had shown his feelings by keeping her safe— hiring a personal guard to protect her from danger when he wasn't there to protect her himself.

He stepped back from the sensual vortex that sucked him closer and closer to her. And just when he'd feared he'd judged her wrong, she'd proved she was a scheming vixen.

His fingers dug into the thirsty towel he'd draped around his neck as he crossed the cool tile floor to her. The sand he tracked in crunched underfoot, but she didn't seem to notice.

She slept soundly, as if she didn't have a care or was exhausted. He suspected the latter when he drew near.

The fading light played over her porcelain features and frail form. His brows slammed together and unease bubbled in his gut, for she was far too pale and far too thin—her simple blouse and slacks hung on her.

The worry she spurred in him infuriated him, for she deserved his fiery wrath, not his concern. He had every reason to hate her. He did hate her!

He despised that she could slumber when sleep had been a stranger to him for six long months.

Yet looking at her roused those tender emotions as well as the memories that never died. He'd seen her a thousand times in his dreams: laughing, flirtatious, sensuous. He'd seen her happy, angry and sad.

But he'd never seen her like this.

She embodied the image of a fragile waif who had washed up on the shore. Far too delicate to wage a battle with him.

And this reunion would be a battle, for he'd not capitulate to her desires. No. He'd vowed to make her regret her callous disregard of their daughter, and her marriage vows.

He leaned close to shake her awake then froze when he saw the picture frame clutched to her chest. *¡Dios mio!* She dared to cradle Cristobel's picture to her heart?

He lurched back and scrubbed a shaky hand over his face, torn between ripping the framed picture from her or taking her in his arms. Did the memories that tormented him do so to her as well? Was she needled with regret?

The streaks of mascara on her pale cheeks confirmed she'd shed recent tears. He had that satisfaction of knowing she'd been touched with grief.

But her remorse came far too late.

She'd brought about the destruction of their marriage and their family the day she cast her vows aside. She'd proved to him that he'd been right to hold a part of himself from her.

For instead of remaining in Cancún to share their grief and see to their daughter's burial, she'd flitted off to England with her lover. She'd forgotten her husband and the baby lying cold in her grave.

But he hadn't forgotten her perfidy.

He jerked the towel from around his neck with a snap and flung it on a nearby chair. Bits of sand peppered the room in a glittering shower of white.

The woman before him stirred, a jerky movement of one coming awake with the knowledge something wasn't quite right. Every nerve in his body snapped and sizzled the second she clearly realized he was standing over her.

Their gazes clashed like angry froth on the shoals.

His blazed with the anger and torment that burned in his soul. Hers opened wide and glinted with apprehension.

He allowed a grim smile. "*Buenos noches, querida.* How good of you to return home at last."

She blinked and sat up quickly, clearly snapping out of her wary spell. "How good of you to be here to greet me." Her lips thinned as she raked his near naked form with a cool, appraising look. "For a change."

It was a clean hit he didn't deserve. *Sí,* he'd spent weeks away from her before their daughter's birth, but he'd needed to put distance between them at a time when her body was lush and tempting him to toss his reservations aside. It was then he had realized the hold she had over his emotions. He knew from past experience that with love came a fear of loss sharp and cold.

So he delved into business. He wasn't about to enlighten his unfaithful wife about his dealings. No, he'd learned that lesson the hard way years ago.

He was a Gutierrez. Like generations before him, he kept his business apart from his family life. It was the only way and she would learn to live with it.

Except she hadn't learned. She'd sought affection in the arms of another man.

"What are you doing here?" she asked.

"There is a tropical storm brewing," he said. "I came to make preparations."

"And swim?"

"*Sí.* The waters are calmer before the storm." Like this reunion with her promised to be?

She looked around the *sala,* the framed photo still clutched tight to her chest. Her brow was creased in confusion or irritation—he didn't care which, for her feelings meant nothing to him.

"You've come here often," she said.

"It is convenient to spend the night here when I'm detained in the city on business." In truth, he came here to reflect on all he'd had in his grasp, and all he'd lost.

"As I recall, you spent more time away from the casa than you did in residence."

He gave a lazy shrug when he felt anything but nonchalant, for the peevish tone that crept into her voice was a barb in his skin—it sounded as if she blamed him for what had happened.

"Why did you come back?" he said.

"Closure."

He waved a negligent hand as if bored. "Meaning?"

She drew in a shaky breath that was at odds with her prim outward show. "I want to visit Cristobel's grave." She gave the room a longing glance. "I wish to sell this house." Her eyes locked with his. "I want a divorce."

He'd expected this, yet the cool order in which she'd delivered her wants chafed him. "Did you go back to your doctor?"

"Of course not."

He believed her. She'd moved past that man. Past him as well. "Our daughter is laid to rest amid her ancestors."

Her throat worked. "I expected she would be, but you can't stop me from visiting my child's grave."

He could if he wished. It would take no more than a

simple request, and Allegra Vandohrn would find herself deported to England.

"I will take you there," he said.

She tensed up at that. "I don't require your company."

"You will have it, regardless."

He waited for her to argue the point. She simply heaved a sigh and gave a shaky nod, but his English rose soon proved she had thorns. "How often have you availed yourself of my house?"

"Whenever I wished to," he said, intrigued by her ire.

"Your arrogance amazes me," she said, the soprano pitch in her contralto voice stopping him. "You could have stayed at a hotel. You could have driven back to your hacienda."

"I chose not to." He kept his expression blank when his insides rampaged with fury, but he welcomed the anger over the other emotions that threatened to blindside him. "I prefer to avoid the crowds at the hotels. As you know, the drive can be treacherous when one is weary or reckless."

That remark drained the color from her face. Her eyes clouded with profound grief. He waited for the satisfaction of besting her to wash over him, of hurting her as she'd hurt him, but all he felt was a vast emptiness that pulsed and throbbed and ached in his soul.

"This is my house," she said simply. "I bought it with my inheritance."

A fact he remembered well, but brushed away with a shrug now. "You have failed to keep up your obligations."

"Uncle Loring said he'd taken care of everything."

Ah, her very proper family to the rescue again. Except this time her uncle had failed her.

"Your housekeeper called me a month after you fled Cancún, wondering what she should do," he said. "Her funds had run out, so I assumed the responsibility."

Profound confusion pulled at her delicate features. "That can't be."

He arched one arrogantly arched eyebrow. "Should I summon the housekeeper to explain?"

"Of course not."

She hugged her tiny waist and he resisted the urge to draw her into his protective embrace. She was his weakness. His Achilles' heel. *¡Dios mio!* Would he always be plagued with concern for this woman?

Her spine went stiff and her features tensed. "Do you bring your women here?"

He just barely bridled his muscles from snapping taut. How dare she ask him that! He stared at the woman he'd vowed to honor until his dying day and swore under his breath.

"Come now, there's no reason to lie—"

"On occasion," he interrupted smoothly.

She looked away, as if the sight of him sickened her, as if hurt by the thought of him bringing another woman here. Strange reaction for the wife who'd taken a lover behind her husband's back. But then their marriage had grown strained the month before Cristobel's birth.

"What of you, *querida?* Did you bring your lover here?"

"How dare you suggest such a thing!"

Her eyes flashed fire even as she seemed to shrink in on herself. Rebellious yet withdrawn. Those two opposites she affected with ease. Those two qualities had lured him to her from the beginning a lifetime ago.

"The only lover I entertained here was you." Her chin came up, her lush lips trembling a fraction before thinning into a disagreeable line. "And do remember you lost the right to call me your darling six months ago."

¡Dios mio! She dared speak to him of rights? She'd shut him out of her life to take up with her lover, then returned to Cancún to portray the affronted one?

He moved in on her, forcing her against the pristine-white wall, bending close to bracket his hands on both sides of her narrow shoulders that quaked despite their rigid lines.

Beads of unease pebbled over her skin, and he just barely caught himself from running a finger over her cool, smooth flesh. Damn, but this woman tied him in knots!

"You should use care before you remind me of what I've lost," he said.

"I've lost, too, Miguel. Surely you realize that!"

She looked away before he could come back with a stinging retort, and it was then that he realized she still clutched the photo of their *niña*. *¡Hostias!* Was that a sob she made?

He pushed away from her like she was poison and dragged his fingers through his damp hair, raking his scalp. He would not feel compassion for her. He would not wish to know she'd suffered a moment, for it would be nothing but lies. He would not care one bit for her. He would not!

Miguel knew the truth. When he'd confronted Loring Vandohrn regarding the whereabouts of his wife, her uncle had informed him that she'd gone on holiday with her lover. He'd suggested Miguel seek a divorce.

It would have been the simplest solution. But a divorce robbed him of vengeance. It did not punish his wife whose recklessness took their child's life. It did not assuage the angst Miguel had lived with for months when he searched for his wife only to be thwarted at every turn.

He looked down at the woman who'd turned his life upside down and wondered why she'd decided to seek a divorce now. Did she wish to marry her lover?

The bead of moisture clinging to her full upper lip confirmed she didn't like him this close to her. God knew it was a mistake for him to tempt fate as well.

It would be so easy for him to dip his head and lap that salty bead of moisture off her mouth. So inviting to trace the lush, provocative bow of her upper lip with his tongue.

Her enticing floral scent teased him with the memory of how much he'd enjoyed making love with this woman—and the countless times since she'd left when he'd reached for her in his sleep.

He hated that weakness for her, that after all that had happened his body still yearned to mesh with the sweet warmth hers offered. The darkening of her pupils proved she wasn't averse to him, either.

Sí, she wanted a divorce? Fine, he'd grant her one after he satisfied his revenge.

"Please, Miguel, just leave me be," she said and turned her face from his.

That would be the sane thing to do. Walk away and not look back. Grant her a divorce and let her have her closure.

But that wouldn't satisfy his vengeance. She'd denied him the satisfaction of confronting her six months ago. Now she'd returned and he'd not be deprived of his just due.

"If that was your wish," he said as he trailed a finger down her pale cheek and felt a shiver of awareness rock her body, "then you should have stayed with your lover."

Her blue eyes snapped with a curious mix of anger and hurt. "Why do you persist in believing the worst of me?"

"You ask that after what you did?"

He pushed away from her then, because he'd never seen her look so miserable.

It was the image he'd tried to envision of her, but seeing it twisted something deep inside him. He hated these feelings she wrought in him. Hated her for making him feel something besides animosity toward her.

"I've had enough. If you won't leave, then I will," she said.

"Running away already?" he asked. "What of this closure you've returned for?"

"I'll never have that as long as I'm subject to your ill temper." She turned away from him and gave a frantic scan of the room, wavering slightly. "Where is the phone?"

"In the bedroom."

She pushed past him without looking at him, seeming not to be looking at anything at all. Though her course was straight, he caught the slight warble in her legs.

He was reminded again by how much weight she'd lost. "Who are you going to call?"

"That's none of your business," she said.

"It is if you're using my phone."

"Very well. I intend to ring for a taxi."

"I will take you where you need to go."

Did she think she could shack up with her lover in Cancún? The paparazzi would have a field day with that gossip.

"I prefer a taxi and a hotel that isn't under your control," she said.

"Then you should have stayed in England."

That brought her facing him again, and this time there was no mistaking her shock. "You've acquired that much power?"

"*Sí,* and I will not have you flaunt a lover under my nose!" He stalked her as a jaguar would a weakened prey, toying with her, knowing he had time to pounce.

She laughed, the sound bitter. "I assure you I do not have a lover here or anywhere."

"You expect me to believe you?"

She whirled on him, her blue eyes snapping with anger now. "I don't care if you do or not."

"You should care, *querida,* for I hold your future in my hands."

Her chin came up, but he caught the slight tremor in it. "Is that a threat?"

He hiked one shoulder in a careless shrug. "A promise. You want a divorce? I'll grant you one."

The wariness was back in her eyes again. "Are you serious?"

"*Sí.* I don't wish to remain married to an unfaithful wife any longer."

"I never broke my vows," she said, seeming angry that he'd insinuate she'd cheated on him.

He smiled, no more than a show of teeth. "*Sí,* you did. I have proof of your infidelity."

"That's impossible!"

"No, *querida,*" he said. "I have pictures, and witnesses."

And now he had the satisfaction of seeing her face leach of color.

CHAPTER TWO

ALLEGRA stared at Miguel, scarcely believing they were having this insane conversation.

"I have spent the past five months in a private sanitarium," she said, remembering every facet of the bland room and the benign gardens visible out her window, painfully mindful of the hours ticking by without word from her husband.

One day smoothly blended into the next, counting off weeks. Months. She knew the sparse staff by serene face and finally by name. Knew what times of the day to expect the doctor, and knew each session would be a struggle to remember the simplest things.

She knew when Sunday rolled around because she'd have a brief visit from Uncle Loring.

That had been the extent of her memory until one month ago. She certainly hadn't had a lover there, or anywhere else for that matter.

"It is called Bartholomew Fields," she said, and meeting his hard gaze, she challenged, "Look it up."

His laugh was a whiplash to her nerves. "So now you are accusing your uncle of lying."

"Of course not. Just what are you insinuating?"

"Your uncle told me you'd gone off on holiday with your lover, *querida.*"

That couldn't be. "Why would he say such a thing?"

"Because it is the truth," he said, the dangerous hiss in his voice raising gooseflesh.

"No, it's not."

After five months, she'd come out of her sleep and begged to see Miguel and her beautiful daughter. That's when the doctor had told her about the tragedy.

Cristobel had died in the auto accident. She'd barely survived herself, losing her memory and her ability to conceive again.

Miguel prowled the room, and she knew he would spring at the slightest provocation. "He suggested I divorce you."

She shook her head, more confused than before. Uncle Loring had been painfully clear in telling her that Miguel held her totally to blame for their daughter's death. He could not bear the sight of her. He wanted nothing more to do with her.

Yet Miguel claimed he'd come after her. Who was she to believe?

The slow, steady thud of her heart told her Miguel was telling the truth. True, her uncle had never liked Miguel, but that was no reason to lie to him about her health.

He was her husband. Then more than ever, she'd needed him at her side.

Instead Miguel had gone back to the Yucatán believing the worst of her. While she'd been locked away at Bartholomew Fields grieving for all she'd lost—her child, her marriage, her sanity.

She'd actually had no desire to go on, until her uncle's health broke and she had to rally her own wits to care for him. It was then that she realized she must heed the doctor's advice and return here for closure.

"I want to see this proof you claim to have," she said, daring him to reveal his hand.

"I will when we reach Hacienda Primaro."

A sliver of fear whispered over Allegra and she shivered. "I'll pass on a visit to your family home."

One dark eyebrow arched high over an eye that glittered hard and unyielding. "It wasn't an invitation, *querida*. You want to see the proof of your indiscretion? It is there in my office. You wish to visit our daughter's grave? She rests in the *cementerio* adjacent to the hacienda."

She looked away and hugged her middle that pulsed with a hollow ache. The trepidation of returning to the hacienda unnerved her.

Something dreadful had happened there, for the apprehension dancing over her skin was real. But what? That memory was lost in the black void, and willing it to become clear in her mind only left her with a dull headache.

"Fine," she said, capitulating without argument. "I will visit the hacienda and Cristobel's grave, then return here."

"No." The single word cracked with finality, defying argument.

Her gaze shifted to Miguel standing tall and imposing in the *sala*. For the first time she noted the changes in him. He'd put on more muscle in his shoulders and torso, making him look formidable. Dangerous even.

He was not a man to be crossed.

Yet she didn't fear him.

No, there was a mystique in his dark eyes that drew her. But though she'd fallen into his arms before, she'd not make that mistake again.

Never again would she allow herself to be shut out of her husband's life. She certainly wouldn't push her heart out there to be trampled again.

"You can't order me about," she said.

He inclined his head in arrogant agreement. "I would not attempt to, but if you wish to have an uncontested divorce, you will agree to my proposal."

The dread in her stomach quivered and knotted, for his threat was clear—agree with him or spend years litigating her divorce. She didn't have the funds for that and he knew it.

Still, she wasn't about to capitulate immediately. "I can't imagine why you'd wish to draw this out."

His flash of teeth warned her she'd not like his answer. "Let's call it equitable compensation for the fortune in jewelry you stole."

She blinked, certain she hadn't heard him right. "I don't know what you're talking about."

"Of course you would deny it." He prowled the room with lazy insouciance, though his glittering eyes continued to skewer her to the spot. "I will admit this was partly my fault, for I gave you the combination to the safe. I trusted you."

The accusation she'd stolen anything from him fired her anger. Though the memory of the hours surrounding the accident remained a blur, she knew she'd not availed herself of anything stored in the safe before she'd left the hacienda.

She felt certain that wherever she was going hadn't warranted her wearing a fortune in jewelry. "All that I took with me that day were my wedding rings."

He stared at her bare left hand. "Did you hock those as well?"

"I didn't pawn any jewelry," she said, hurt and angry that he continued to believe the worst in her.

"You still have them then?"

"I told you all I had with me were my wedding rings."

He loosed a raw laugh. "Which you no longer wear."

She stared at the stubborn man she'd lost her heart to and weighed her actions. Really, there was no choice.

"In this, I take delight in proving you wrong," she said.

Allegra pulled on the gold chain hidden under her blouse until the diamond and emerald engagement ring and gold wedding band that had been created for her dangled free. "I lost a good deal of weight and feared I'd lose these."

His long, lean fingers closed over the rings that were warmed from nestling between her breasts. A quicksilver glint of longing lit his dark eyes then vanished under his shrewd scrutiny.

"You expect me to believe you wear these all the time?"

"I couldn't care less what you believe!" She gave the chain a tug, and he released the rings as if they burned him. "Perhaps it was silly of me to continue wearing the tokens of your troth when it is clear you no longer wanted me."

"I never said I didn't want you, *querida*." A slow rapacious smile curved the lips that had once ravished every inch of her body, and despite her annoyance with Miguel a tingling heat skittered over her body.

"Enough arguing," she said. "Our prenuptial agreement details my settlement. I've no desire to contest it."

"It would be a waste of time and money to do so."

A fact she was well aware of. "Fine," she said again when she felt anything but fine. "What is your proposal?"

"I want you."

Those three words sucked the breath from her. Surely he couldn't mean it like that. But as the seconds pounded by and he failed to explain, she suspected this was indeed intended to be a sexual connotation.

"Want me how?" she asked anyway in case her foggy mind was imagining things.

And right now her imagination was running horribly wild. Just the idea of falling into his strong arms again was a temptation she found difficult to reject.

The carnal glint in his eyes threatened to melt her remaining resolve. "As my wife. My lover."

His words flowed through her veins in a thick, warm rush of need. She should be offended he'd suggest such a thing— at the very least she should be angry he'd demote her to the role of mistress.

But the idea hummed through her senses and made her feel more alive than she had in months. For the life of her, she couldn't think of a solid argument to throw out there.

In fact she was suddenly having difficulty dragging her gaze away from the solid expanse of his bare chest. Her fingertips tingled with the need to trace the hard slabs of muscle liberally sprinkled with black hair.

His bronzed skin would be warm and the hair soft as down. Her gaze tracked the hair that narrowed into a thin band and disappeared under his swim trunks that he wore indecently low on his lean hips.

For the first time since the accident, moisture gathered in the juncture of her thighs. Yes, she'd missed her husband. She'd missed the unbridled sex they'd shared. Missed lying in his arms afterward listening to the steady drum of his heart.

"A farewell fling then," she said, and cringed at the reedy pitch to her voice that seemed to scream of her own need. "What if I refuse?"

"Then the deal is off. I'll drag the divorce out and slap a lien against your beach house." He crossed to her, each step slow and measured and tightening her nerves until she thought they'd snap.

Her mouth dropped open, and a sick feeling expanded in her belly to pop her sensual bubble. "You'd do that to me?"

"In a heartbeat," he said with arrogant assurance of his power. "What will it be?"

There was only one choice and he knew it. The only difference was her reason for bending to his will—she wanted closure badly enough to put her heart through an emotional wringer with Miguel again.

"When do we begin?"

"Tonight. I invited a *norteamericano* businessman to dinner tonight to show my gratitude for the property we have successfully negotiated." He ran a finger down her flushed cheek and she had to lock her knees to keep from bowing into him. "The El Trópico in Playa del Carmen would be the perfect place for dinner and drinks."

She pulled back and stared at his arrogantly handsome face, expecting a glint of reluctance or hopefully humor after tossing out that name. But his features were too remote for her to read.

"Are you serious?" she asked. "The Quinta Avenida at night is a swarm of tourists, celebrities wishing to be seen and paparazzi."

He smiled and not a kind one. "Afraid your lover will see us together on the cover of a slick rag, *querida?* Or has your romance with Amando Rivera ended?"

"Amando! You can't believe I'd court his interest."

His gaze blazed into hers with brutal intensity. "I know you did."

"No! It wasn't like that."

"It was exactly like that," he said. "I know where and why you secretly met with him. When you left the hacienda that last day, so did he."

A dark memory of that day teased her mind and was gone, leaving her trembling with uncertainty and fear. Yes, she'd worked with Amando at first to help Miguel.

But it had changed. All she was certain of was she had an intense dislike for the guard Miguel had hired to protect her.

"Wear something slinky," he said as she passed him on legs that still quaked and entered the bedroom they'd shared.

"I've no idea if I have anything suitable," she said.

He waved a hand in the general direction of the bedroom, the movement sensuously masculine and dismissive as he punched in numbers on his mobile phone. "There is a red gown that would be perfect."

She went absolutely still as those words replayed in her mind, triggering a memory she'd forgotten. If it was the same dress— But it must be. She'd bought it at Miguel's insistence.

How could she have let that memory slip from her?

The question pinged her mind as she crossed to the closet, hearing the timbre of his voice rattling off Spanish but too engrossed in having captured a lost memory than to eavesdrop on his conversation.

She ran a shaky hand through her hair, remembering the shopping excursion as clearly as if it'd just happened. He'd taken her to an elite shop nearly one year ago, for the functions he'd be attending that fall demanded that his mistress be decked out to the nines.

Though he never told her what she could or couldn't wear, it was obvious he preferred elegant fashions over slinky ones. Since she wasn't comfortable wearing revealing fashions, it was a perfect match.

Until the clerk brought out the red gown and proclaimed it was made for her.

She'd had just enough sips of champagne to take the dare.

And the gown was daring with the front consisting of two gathered swaths of glittery fabric that covered her bosom, and the back bared nearly to the dimples in her bum. It fit like skin, and she'd laughingly told Miguel she'd not be able to wear undergarments with it.

His eyes had blazed so hot they'd chased away her chills.

He'd bought it, and she'd set it aside for the gala that December. But a week later she'd discovered she was pregnant, and by the time the gala came around, her figure no longer fit the daring gown.

"Did you find it?" he asked behind her, his breath warm on her nape.

"Yes." She took it from the closet where it had hung in its protective bag, and her face burned with embarrassment. *Don't look at him. Don't let him know how this dress and his closeness affected her.*

Allegra slipped another hanger off the rod and draped a deep blue gown with generous drapes over the red one. "In case the red one doesn't fit."

"Of course."

Must he stand so close? Must he smell so incredibly male? Must her body choose now to come out of its deep sleep?

What was she thinking by agreeing to do this?

His indecent proposal should infuriate her. It was an insult to their marriage. To her as a woman.

It reduced their marriage that had begun for her with such hope to a purely carnal level.

She should tell him to go to hell and call his bluff. But she couldn't force the words out.

Miguel didn't bluff. He'd drag out their divorce for years, and the emotional toil would ruin her more than the financial loss.

She couldn't let that happen. Besides, the idea of lying in her husband's arms again roused the primitive beast in her— a beast she'd thought she'd never witness again.

Only with Miguel, her heart warned.

She met his steady gaze with a tentative smile. "So this is it? There are no other surprises for me agreeing to do this charade?"

"None." He held his head at an imperious angle, his eyes hooded, his broad shoulders dusted with glittering bits of white sand that she longed to brush off. "I will advise my attorney to begin divorce proceedings tomorrow, and I'll give you fair market value for the beach house at the end of the week."

"One week. That's how long this fling will last?" she asked.

"*Sí*. Did you expect less? More?"

She shook her head, embarrassed to admit she hadn't thought that far ahead. She'd agreed to his outrageous offer without knowing the details.

She knew what that said about her, and so did he.

"You will accompany me everywhere, *querida*."

He smiled a wolf's smile and dropped a kiss on her mouth. So fleeting. So brief she thought she'd simply imagined it.

"Day and night," he said against her lips.

Those last words ribboned through her to tie her emotions in knots. It took every ounce of willpower to keep from leaning into his touch. Just like that and her resolve nearly shattered again.

"Cocktails are at eight," he said, striding toward the master bedroom. "We leave in two hours. Do not be late."

"I wouldn't dream of it," she got out as he flung his towel on the bed and strode toward the shower, shucking his swim trunks with masculine grace.

Thoughts about her inadequate figure swathed in a gown that left nothing to the imagination left her. Her gaze swept down his beautifully bronzed sculpted body, admiring his muscular back, narrow hips, tight bum and long, long legs.

Warmth spread over her like the first fingers of a new dawn cresting the horizon. Heat as thick and hot as lava flowed through her veins.

As before, Miguel was fire in her veins. She'd never lusted for a man as she had him, and she certainly hadn't expected to feel the same charged energy course through her again, not after all they'd been through.

But it was there—stronger than before.

She bolted up the stairs to the guest room and blocked everything from her mind but getting through this night. She'd returned for closure and she'd have it. If going through the motions of marriage with Miguel was the only means to achieve it, then so be it.

She'd suffered the worst life had to hand her when her darling daughter had died. She'd managed to push past the grief and remorse.

She could certainly do what Miguel wanted of her and not lose her dignity or her pride. And if he captured her heart again?

Well, she'd been through that, too, and survived.

After a quick shower that refreshed her spirits somewhat, she stepped into the crimson gown and took an appraising look at her reflection. The style was more risqué than she'd recalled, but her weight loss was an asset to the design. She'd never aspired to have a model's figure, but she had one now.

Fortunately the gown hid the scar marking her surgery. What would Miguel think when he saw it? Would he still want her?

She pinched her eyes shut and loosed a groan of disgust. It didn't matter what he thought of her body. She was his paramour for one week.

Nothing more. Nothing less.

She ran the brush through her mass of hair, then twisted it into a simple chignon. A bit of makeup and she stepped back to take stock of herself. She heaved a sigh, pleased she'd donned the image of the sophisticated wife of a billionaire.

All she needed now was the courage to carry her downstairs and throw herself into the role of his wife that she'd vowed to assume until her dying day. It should be easy, since she'd discovered one vital thing hadn't changed.

She was still in love with her husband.

CHAPTER THREE

MIGUEL stood by the window and stared out to sea, but still only saw the hunger in Allegra's blue eyes when he'd tossed out his proposition. He'd thought she'd balk when she realized he'd set them up to be targets of the gossip rags. He'd expected anger at being forced to do his bidding in order to gain her freedom.

But she hadn't hesitated long before agreeing to resume the role of his wife, leaving him to believe that she wanted out of their marriage so badly that she'd prostitute herself.

She was a money-grabbing schemer. She'd likely run through the funds she'd gained by selling the jewelry she'd stolen and was desperate to sell the beach house to fund her affair. Was Amando Riveras waiting for her to return to him with a fat purse, or had she taken a new lover?

That possibility was a fresh knife thrust in his heart. He hated her as hotly as he'd once desired her for taking his child when she ran off with her lover, for her defiance ended his *niña*'s life. He'd been sure her deceit had burned out all feelings in him save vengeance.

But being with her again, drawing in her provocatively sweet scent, being close enough to run his hands through her wealth of hair and glide his palms over her creamy soft skin had reawakened the unbridled lust she'd always ignited in him.

She was the spark to his tinder, and he was powerless to put out the flames of desire.

He prided himself on his steely control—until he'd met her. She was the enigma that slipped past his defenses. She was the waif who stole into his thoughts when he needed his rapier wits about him.

She was the one person who struck fear in him, for the feelings she roused terrified him more than the very real possibility of something ill befalling her.

Even now he caught himself concerned about her drastic weight loss that went beyond her losing her baby weight. He knew well she'd always fussed about being too heavy when he'd thought her perfect.

Now she had the figure to rival a fashion model. The pale fragile complexion was indicative of someone who'd spent an exorbitant amount of time indoors. *In bed with Amando?*

He swore and ran a hand over his just-shaved jaw as he thought of his wife making love with the man he'd hired to guard her. How long had it taken for the man to seduce Allegra?

The attraction had to have taken root before she gave birth to Cristobel. While her belly was swollen with *his* child, the man he'd handpicked to guard his wife from a kidnapper had seduced her.

And she'd welcomed Amando's attentions!

He'd known Allegra was unhappy with their marriage those past few months. She hated living at Hacienda Primaro. She had argued bitterly with his *madre*. She complained about being shut out of his life and wished to hold a position within his corporation.

"A Gutierrez wife does not work in that sense," he'd told her. "Your job is your home and family."

"I'll go crazy here with so little to do," she'd insisted.

He refused to be moved. "Then perhaps you should ask Madre what causes you could lend your name and time to."

She'd said no more about holding a job after that. He'd thought she'd finally understood her position.

But he'd been wrong.

While he was immersed in helping the indigenous people survive a catastrophe, she was stealing a fortune in jewels and leaving him with the man he'd hired to protect her from kidnappers.

Miguel had returned to Hacienda Primaro to find his wife gone, his daughter dead and his marriage over. She'd flown back to England, not even staying for their *niña*'s burial.

Over the ensuing months, his mind had conjured up a thousand scenarios of her and Amando secreted away. He spent countless sleepless nights envisioning ways to make her pay for carelessly endangering their daughter's life, and for dragging him through this emotional hell.

Miguel had been on the verge of hiring a detective to find her when her housekeeper in Cancún called him. Allegra had phoned to have her ready the beach house.

He made sure he was here waiting for her.

He squinted at the dark line gathering on the horizon. Would he find peace of mind after he extinguished the vengeance that burned in him night and day? Would he ever be free of the guilt that battered his heart because he'd not been there to stop his wife from leaving with his darling *niña*?

He tipped his head back and stared at the pristine-white ceiling where a fan gently stirred the air that was rife with tension. He'd paid off this house for her as her bride's gift.

Their love nest, she'd called it.

It had been, too, for they'd retreated here when they needed to be alone. They'd created their beautiful *niña* here.

Unease rippled over his skin. If she'd wanted out of her

marriage, why hadn't she asked for a divorce before? Why the hell hadn't she left Cristobel with Madre when she ran off with Amando Riveras?

The scuff of a shoe on the steps alerted him to her entrance. Before the accident, he always turned to greet her with a welcoming smile that mirrored his desire, always had been stunned by her natural beauty. Her poise. Her sensual aura that enveloped him in her white-hot woman's heat.

They'd had a passionate connection that he'd never felt with another woman. It caught him off guard to discover that attraction was still there—still as commanding as it had been that first day he'd seen her on the beach.

But he wouldn't let her know that. She'd lost that right to know what was in his heart when she left him for another man.

Miguel faced her, his features carefully wiped clean of the emotions that kept him on edge. The erotically sensual woman before him made his pulse race.

Even wearing such a provocative gown, she looked poised and sure of herself. Surely every man would lust after her tonight.

"You are more alluring in that gown than I remember," he said.

The flush streaking across her cheeks and coloring her throat reminded him of the day he'd bought this dress for her. She'd blushed and fussed and told him that it would be months before she could fit into this gown because she'd just discovered she was pregnant.

That day he'd started thinking of forever with this woman instead of an affair. That day he'd thought with his heart instead of his head, even though a part of him warned of the danger of caring too deeply for her.

He wanted her, and was certain he'd not fall that deeply under her spell. But he had.

He'd been terrified of loving her. And terrified of losing her.

In the end he'd done both.

He cut a sharp glance at his watch, blotting the provocative sight of her from his mind. Yet his body still hummed with awareness of her.

He gritted his teeth and tamped down the raw animal need coursing through him. She came back for closure?

Fine, he'd gladly help her slam the door on their past. But she was in for a rude shock, for when he was done with her, she'd have nothing. She'd gotten all she was going to get from his family.

No, that was a lie. He'd lived for the moment when the business dinner was concluded, when he and Allegra returned here tonight. When she upheld her agreement to be his wife in all ways. When he took her heart again. And when he dumped her as she had him, she'd know the pain of betrayal.

He let his gaze sweep up her, slowly this time, noting the tensing in her limbs and inviting swell of her bosom. The telling hip thrust was a primitive and provocative invitation for him to push her against the wall and take her now.

Sí, she was a temptress. He ruthlessly tamped down his urges and shifted to ease the ache of his arousal.

Tonight he'd indulge in what she offered.

Tonight she'd be his to command. To conquer.

"Where is your jewelry?" he asked, his deep voice startling her from admiring the refined gentleman standing before her.

Miguel had told her once that his Spanish ancestors had come to Mexico to conquer it. That one conquistador had seduced a Mayan princess yet settled here, joining two worlds, two cultures.

His grandfather had achieved great wealth. His father had capitalized on it to increase the fortune. But it was Miguel's cunning and daring that propelled the family holdings well into the exalted group of billionaires.

He was a conquistador, his bearing proud and unflinching. His jawline was strong, the cheekbones high and pronounced. He had a straight aristocratic nose, and his dark mocha eyes glittered with a mesmerizing light that burned from within.

But the feature she'd loved most about Miguel was the shape of his mouth. The lower lip was full and curved just so. The upper one had a generous bow that arched as if hinting he was always amused.

Or mocking, as he seemed now.

Allegra stuffed a few essentials into an evening bag, annoyed his spicy scent wrapped around her like loving arms. It annoyed her that he'd brought up the subject of jewelry.

She turned her left hand so he could see her rings. She'd found tape in a cabinet in the loo and added enough to keep her rings from falling off her fingers.

"The gold chain did nothing for the gown," she said, when his dark gaze fixed on hers again.

She'd left her jewelry at the hacienda. She didn't miss the extravagant pieces that had passed down through his family, for the designs dripping with gems had never appealed to her. But she mourned the loss of those few items, especially the emerald suspended on a delicate gold chain, that he'd given her after she'd told him she was pregnant.

A sacred bond, he'd called it. Green gems held special meaning for the Mayan, so it was only fitting that they commemorate their union with an emerald, and mark the conception of their firstborn daughter with one as well.

His thick eyebrows slanted, his gaze appraising, his stance domineering. "Perhaps the effect is better without adornments."

"Whether it is or not, this will have to do." She lifted her chin. "Are we ready then?"

"*Sí.* My car is in the garage." He grasped her arm, his touch firm and warm. Commanding yet intimate.

She moved with him in silent synchronization, a woman clearly attune to her man's slightest nuances. The months apart hadn't changed that.

The sense of oneness they projected drew attention. They'd always made a striking couple, whether they consciously tried or not. They were just that in sync with each other's moods and desires.

Now was no different. But the image they projected was a scam.

He was angry. Furiously so.

Well, she was annoyed, too. Nothing had changed. He still regarded her as an adornment on his arm.

Like everything else he owned, she'd been a possession. But was that why she'd left him? She hoped she'd find the answers here soon.

She proceeded him through the side door into the garage, expecting to find the luxury sedan that he favored for long road trips. A sports car sat in its place, as sleek and black as the jaguar that bore its name.

As dangerous as the man escorting her into it and then striding around the hood with masculine grace and climbing behind the wheel.

"Is something wrong?" he asked when he caught her staring at him.

The list was long, but she shook her head in answer. What difference did it make that she was an uneasy passenger after the accident?

It was just another of the crosses she had to bear. She fastened her seat belt, somewhat surprised when he did the same for he'd never done so before.

He zipped out of the garage and onto the road, then threw

the car in gear and sped off. The jolt pressed Allegra against the seat, and for a moment she felt a spate of panic that had haunted her since that night.

She steadied her breathing and focused on the diverse scenery as they zipped down Carretera 307, the jungle to her right and the expanse of white sand beaches to her left.

This was one of the most beautiful places on earth, yet tonight she was so filled with apprehension that she feared it would take little provocation for her to jump out of her skin.

"Having second thoughts?" he asked.

"No," she said, taking small pleasure that he'd picked up on her unease.

At least she hadn't been wrong about that affinity with Miguel! But it also meant she'd have the devil's time hiding her emotions from him.

"Relax and enjoy the drive."

"I'm trying to." She pressed her palms flat against her thighs and drew in several calming breaths.

"How is your mother?" she asked to fill the silence.

"Busy with her grandson," he said.

"Your sister's son was a precocious child," she said, and bit back adding he was spoiled and rude.

He nodded as he wove in and out of traffic. "He enjoys having all of Madre's attention."

"That will change when another grandchild is born," she said, certain Miguel's sister would have more.

But Miguel would likely remarry and start a new family one day. She ignored the stab of pain that thought wrought.

Even if they could overcome their differences, even if they could come to trust one another one day, one fact remained to make her totally unsuitable as his wife. She couldn't have any more children, and a man in Miguel's position would want heirs.

"*Sí*, it will be a big adjustment for him," he said, and she responded with a murmur of agreement.

She took the time to study Miguel, noting the new lines in his face. The sharper glint in his eyes. The somber expression that hinted he always had something troubling him.

A flicker of light behind them caught her eye. She looked back just as a car swerved sharply inches from their bumper.

"No!"

She shielded her face, expecting the air bag to explode into her. A cry sliced above the scream of tires, the sound crackling with agony and terror.

He whipped the car to the side of the highway and fishtailed on the narrow shoulder as he brought the car to a dead stop.

"Allegra!" He grabbed her arms and forced them down.

She blinked at him then stared into the rear seat, her mouth dry, her breath no more than a flutter. "Oh God, I thought—"

She couldn't go on, couldn't force the words out.

"You thought what?" he said, a quaver creeping into his deep voice as his hands glided up and down her suddenly chilled arms. "Tell me."

"I thought that car was going to hit us." She closed her eyes and forced herself to take metered breaths to still her racing heart. "Like before."

"What do you mean?"

"The accident."

A tense silence vibrated between then.

"A car hit you?" An incredulous rake of his gaze followed his question that echoed with skepticism.

She shook her head, annoyed her memory was littered with holes. "I don't know. I hear the explosion of the airbags and the suffocating pressure on my chest. I hear Cristobel crying."

"What do you remember?" he asked.

"Very little. What I do recall comes in snippets that often seem out of order."

"You suffer from a memory loss?" he asked, incredulity ringing loud and clear in his voice.

"Yes, a form of amnesia," she said. "Didn't Uncle Loring explain?"

His dark brows slammed into a vee over the aristocratic blade of his nose. "Not one word."

Allegra didn't know what to make of that. If Miguel was to be believed, her uncle had lied to him about her condition and her whereabouts. Why would he do such a thing?

"How often do you have these flashbacks?" he asked, a note of concern creeping into his voice now.

Most nights, or any of the other triggers she hadn't anticipated that caught her off guard. "Often enough, though of late the same snippets have played over and over." She looked into his eyes then and said simply, "The accident and two weeks following it are a mystery to me."

His dark eyes flared with surprise, but the strong hand that closed protectively over hers was her undoing. For he didn't merely touch her. His thumb stroked her hand, and the warm vital connection between them brought back vibrant memories of the time when they'd merely sit close and hold hands.

She'd mourned that link with Miguel nearly as much as she grieved over her daughter's death. But too soon he released her and scowled out the windshield, and the darkening of his tanned cheeks hinted he disliked revealing that much of his feelings to her.

"How long do they think this block will last?" he asked.

"The doctor said it could last a day or forever," she said, which was the reason she'd decided to leave Bartholomew Fields.

She was suffocating under the doctor's watchful eye. She

hadn't wanted to be dependent on others for the rest of her life, so she dug deep for the gumption to take matters into her own hands.

It was clear nobody else was coming to her defense. Not her uncle. Certainly not her husband.

"I believed what I was told," she said. "Just like you did."

"What is that supposed to mean?"

"You gave up on us, Miguel," she said. "If you'd really wanted to find me, I wouldn't have been a virtual prisoner in Bartholomew Fields."

Her charge rose as a wall between them, for she knew he could move mountains if he chose to. He hadn't tried hard enough to find her. He'd given up on her.

He swore under his breath and jerked back behind the wheel, but instead of throwing the car into gear, he reached into his pocket and withdrew his mobile. "I will call Señor McClendon and give our regrets for tonight."

"Don't."

She laid a hand atop his and jolted when a intense bolt of emotion shot from him into her. Anger. Confusion. Empathy.

"You need to rest," he said. "The trip taxed you."

"I'm all right." She'd done nothing but rest for months. "There is no reason to postpone your dinner."

He tipped his head to the side and studied her, as if he was gauging if he could trust her to pull this off. He likely suspected she'd flake-out and embarrass him in front of the paparazzi that were sure to be present.

"If you are feeling—" he paused, as if searching for the right word to describe her spell "—unnerved, then we should postpone this evening until you are more in control of your emotions."

"I'm fine," she lied. "There's no need to alter your plans for tonight."

His critical assessment of her screamed disagreement. "You are certain of this?"

"Yes," she said, though she wasn't sure of anything.

She'd let her uncle handle things when she was hospitalized. Now it seemed that he'd lied to her, and he'd lied to Miguel.

Why would Uncle Loring keep her from Miguel? She could only guess that he'd sought to protect her from an uncaring husband.

She curled her fingers into her palms, angry over the lost time apart, the lost memories she may never recover. Most of all, it angered her that they'd lost the chance to cling to each other in the face of tragedy.

She glanced at Miguel. He drummed his fingers on the steering wheel and scowled out the windshield. She knew he was on the verge of taking her back to the beach house because he doubted her stamina.

She refused to be locked away from life or cower before the paparazzi. She'd come back to the Yucatán for closure, but now she wanted answers as well.

"Do you intend to sit here all night staring out the window, or are we going to Playa del Carmen for dinner?" she asked.

His gaze flicked to hers, and the hot challenge simmering there made her breath catch.

"We join the *Tejanos* as planned. Hold on." He'd jutted out into traffic as he spoke, as if testing her to see if she'd lose her grip on reality again.

She dug her fingernails into the leather seat and cast him a sideways look. A muscle ticked madly in his lean cheek. Some perceived that tic as anger, but she knew better. It was the only visible sign she'd seen that belied he was nervous.

She suspected a good deal of it was his aversion toward the paparazzi he'd decided to court this night. But had her barb truly hit a nerve? Could he possibly feel guilty for not finding her?

More likely she'd tweaked his formidable pride by tossing the truth back in his face. He'd not wanted her anymore.

She'd known that when she'd come back here. Still, she'd left the safe haven her doctor offered to confront the most exciting man she'd ever met.

Time would tell if it was a choice she'd live to regret.

CHAPTER FOUR

DARE he believe Allegra suffered amnesia following the accident?

That certainly hadn't been an act meant to dupe him when she'd whipped around and stared into the rear seat. The terror on her face had been too real—her skin too pale, her eyes distant and filled with an anguish that sent chills careening down his spine.

No, that hadn't been an act.

His body leaped into full protective mode the second he realized her fear was genuine. If she hadn't been strapped in her seat, he was sure she would have thrown herself into his arms.

His open arms, for he was reaching to gather her close at that same moment. Even now after her terror had passed and she seemed in control, he sensed a vulnerability in her that kept his nerves dancing on the razor's edge.

He was compelled to believe she'd been injured in the accident even though he knew that wasn't the case at all. For if she had suffered an injury great enough to cause amnesia, his *madre* would have informed him after the accident. He rued the fact he had been out of country, unable to see the truth for himself.

No, Allegra had walked away from the accident and left

Cancún with Amando a mere two days after the accident. She left the care of their daughter's interment to his *madre*. She hadn't even had the decency to attend the funeral!

Bearing those truths in mind was the impetus he needed to gain the upper hand over those tender emotions he reviled.

As for her memory loss, he suspected Allegra had suffered another accident while she was off with her lover. Perhaps her guilt over what she'd done had been so great that she truly believed she'd been injured in the same accident that took their daughter's life.

If so, then it was fitting, but not nearly punishment enough for what she'd done to their innocent daughter.

He wanted her to hurt as badly as he did. He wanted her to realize she could not cuckold him and walk away without repercussions.

"Okay," he said, "We proceed as planned."

"Okay." She nodded.

When he married Allegra, he'd vowed to love, trust and protect her. But he'd failed on all counts.

That admission lashed him like his ancestor's cat-o'-nine tails. He'd professed to love her, yet he'd held a part of himself back from her. He'd vowed to honor her, yet he'd hired a man to watch her in his stead.

He'd entrusted others to keep her safe while he threw himself into shoring up his empire. He'd left her and his child alone and clearly she'd grown bored.

Sí, he'd given her ample reasons to take a lover and leave him. He'd given her damn few to stay.

He drove the Jaguar up the palm lined driveway and whipped beneath the *palapa* at the El Trópico and parked, giving the valet the barest nod as he climbed from the car. He took a moment to adjust his tie and rein in his anger while another valet rushed to assist the lady.

Allegra stepped from the car and swayed slightly, as if caught unaware by the increasing wind pushing in from the Caribbean. The innate sense that her unsteadiness wasn't an affectation had him rounding the hood of the car.

He was at her side in seconds, his palm cupping her elbow.

¡Maldita sea! Forcing her to go through with this now wasn't a good idea. As soon as the thought crossed his mind, he swore again.

He would not be swayed by tears or woebegone glances that made his heart stutter. But he wouldn't make a public spectacle out of her, either.

"You do not appear well," he said, his voice pitched for her ears alone.

"I'm fine."

She leaned into him as she had countless times, and his arm went around her narrow shoulders to anchor her to him.

It was a natural coming together that only lovers could orchestrate. The fit was perfect. The touch, the scent, the feel of her head tucked beneath his chin sent an electrifying jolt through him.

He was gripped with a tightening awareness of her as a woman. *His* woman!

The first blinding flash of a camera caught him by surprise. He blinked and turned to shield Allegra from the glare as more cameras flashed around them in angry starbursts.

"Let's get inside," he said.

He escorted her through the glass doors into the lavish lobby of the hotel, leaving the paparazzi to content themselves with the few shots they'd gotten. They'd serve the purpose, thanks to his instincts kicking in.

The headlines would question if she was back in his life to stay. The images would reflect him protecting her—a clear sign to Amando Riveras that his machinations had failed to hold her.

Yet even as that proprietary thought crossed his mind, a more unsettling one dampened this coup. There was a time not too long ago when he and Allegra presented the same image.

He'd believed his marriage strong. Believed his wife was content. Yet she left him without warning.

She kept pace with him as they crossed the carpeted expanse toward the Italian restaurant he and Allegra had favored. Its small private dining room made it perfect for this meeting.

More heads turned as they walked through the waiting room, and why wouldn't they considering the way her red gown molded over the soft swells of her breasts and hugged her firm bottom?

She was upholding her part of their agreement without hesitation. That was what he must remember to keep his libido in check.

The headwaiter jumped to attention the second Miguel and Allegra stepped in the door.

"*Buenos noches,* Señor and Señora Gutierrez," the man said, as if it hadn't been nine months since he and Allegra had dined here together. "Please follow me to the Xaman Room."

"*Gracias,* Ferdinand," he said. "Has Señor and Señora McClendon arrived?"

"*Sí, señor.* Perhaps five minutes ago."

Miguel would have preferred to be here to greet the businessman from Texas as a host should. But he'd lost control with Allegra, and that episode had wasted precious time. He glanced at her now, arrested by her beauty and poise.

No, she outwardly appeared composed. He felt the tremors rocking through her. Her serenity was a thin facade.

There was precious little he could do about it now. The millionaire he'd struck a lucrative deal with was here, accompanied by his daughter. Once they sat through a dinner and exchanged pleasantries, he'd take Allegra back to the beach house.

The paparazzi would have a field day with their arrival. That is all he'd hoped to achieve tonight.

The heaviness in his groin disagreed. He wanted her tonight, and there was nothing stopping him.

Miguel slid his hand to the small of Allegra's back to guide her into the private dining room. His palm glided over her smooth, silken skin.

The gesture was one he'd done countless times, yet at this moment it felt new and tantalizing. Was the tremor he felt in her borne of surprise, or did the same desire touch her?

Even if they had entered the room without the *Tejanos'* notice, now wasn't the time to discuss intimacies.

"*Buenos noches,* Señor McClendon." Miguel turned to the *Tejano*'s daughter and inclined his head. "Señorita McClendon," he added. "My apologies for arriving late."

"Better late than never, Miguel." Tara McClendon plucked the skewered olive from her glass with perfectly manicured fingers and slipped the fruit between her lips in a provocative gesture he found offensive.

Her slinky black gown fit her like a second skin, revealing an artfully tanned body devoid of any excess fat. A gold chain circled the slender column of her throat, and from it hung a large solitaire that nestled in her cleavage.

Her gaze fixed on Miguel's, and the invitation in her pale eyes was bold and lurid. *Sí,* she always made it obvious she'd welcome his attention, and a glance hinted the *Tejano* didn't seem aware of his daughter's flirtations.

Allegra noticed, though. She tensed beside him. He'd always found that spate of jealousy in her unnecessary before, for he'd given her no reason to believe he'd stray.

He inclined his head toward the *Tejano* and his daughter in turn. "Señor and Señorita McClendon, allow me to introduce *mi esposa*, Allegra."

"Nice to meet you, *señora*." The *Tejano* swallowed Allegra's hand in his much larger one, his somber look putting Miguel on alert. "I was mighty sorry to hear about that accident. My condolences."

"Thank you," Allegra said, her tone polite, her smile brief but gracious as she extracted her hand from his.

"Miguel, you didn't tell us you were still married," Tara said, her full lips pulling into a pout.

He gave a shrug of impatience. "I keep my personal life apart from business."

The *Tejano*'s daughter smiled. "Spoken like a man who guards his secrets well."

As well she knew! The way Allegra looked from Tara to him convinced him that she'd recognized the familiarity between them.

"You know, if it'd been anyone but your husband, I'd never have parted so easily with those old sisal haciendas," McClendon said and favored Allegra with a conspiratorial wink.

"You are friends then?" she asked.

McClendon gave a good-natured laugh. "I've known him since he was a boy."

Yet the *Tejano* had haggled over the price to the point Miguel's patience had nearly snapped. "If you, *señor*, weren't an old friend of my father's, I would have called off negotiations months ago."

"How long did it take to solidify this deal?" Allegra asked.

McClendon scrubbed a beefy hand along his ruddy jaw. "Reckon it took close to seven months."

Allegra's smile was as tense as her spine, but it was the pain in the wide eyes that clashed with his that hit him like a gut punch. "So this was the business deal that took so much of your time."

He inclined his head once in answer, unwilling to say more

in front of the McClendons. Like his father, he was careful to keep business and family apart.

In fact he was more guarded about it because he didn't want his wife to interfere in his business dealings as his *madre* had done.

Tara McClendon struck a siren's pose by the window, but her action screamed calculating artifice. "What I can't understand," she said as she lifted a martini off a tray, "is why are you willing to trade three fabulous hotels for those run-down plantations?"

"Competing with the Riviera Maya crowd lost its allure," Miguel said.

"But renovating old haciendas appeals to you?" Tara asked.

"*Sí,*" he said as he assisted Allegra into her chair. Her subtle floral fragrance was a more powerful aphrodisiac than Tara McClendon's intensely exotic scent.

She'd caught her hair up in a knot of sorts, but a few strands trailed down the slender column of her neck. If he bent a bit more, he could press his lips to skin that would be warm and soft.

Sí, he'd lost his appeal for the resort life, but not for the woman he'd found on the beach.

"The properties complement the historic haciendas I've already renovated into luxury hotels and resorts, and preserve a rich part of history," Miguel said.

"Going to cost you a fortune to restore them," McClendon said.

Miguel shrugged off the concern about cost. The properties were the legacy he'd hoped to pass down to his children, he admitted as he took his place beside his wife. Even after the tragedy, he remained determined to increase his empire for his family he'd have one day.

His *madre* repeatedly advised him to divorce Allegra and find a proper wife now. A woman who would be content to delve into worthy efforts befitting a *señora* of her station. A woman who would give him children and accept that she had no place in a man's world.

He slid a glance at his wayward wife.

She looked everywhere but at him, but he suspected the McClendons were too busy ordering their dinners to notice her pique. The fact she seemed annoyed with him wasn't a surprise.

Perhaps she was upset that he'd been negotiating with McClendon for six months or more. But he wasn't in the habit of explaining his actions to anyone.

Business was business, and family was family. The two did not mix.

The waitress opened the door to leave and an ice-blond *niña* darted into the room in a rush of giggly effervescence. Her blue eyes sparkled with life, and her laughter bubbled clear and infectious.

His chest tightened with longing. What would Cristobel have been like at this age?

"I'm so sorry." A woman rushed in after the girl and swept the laughing child up in her arms.

Red-faced, she left mumbling another apology, but the child's laughter remained. To be that free and happy—

The *Tejano* chuckled. "Kids are the same the world over."

"*Sí.*" His gaze flicked to Allegra.

The longing in her eyes took his breath away, for in that split second there was no doubt she still grieved for their daughter, too.

McClendon lifted his whiskey and water in a toast. "Here's to big families and providing the means for the next generation to make their mark on the world."

Miguel's blood flowed thick and hot at the thought of fathering a legacy. *Sí,* one day he'd remarry and sire children. One day he'd start a family again.

He glanced at Allegra and noted the worry pulling at her artfully arched brows. Surely she didn't think he intended to start over again with her?

"¡Salud!" Miguel said, gaining supreme satisfaction when Allegra's smiled wavered and her cheeks flushed a telling pink.

Allegra's head throbbed by the time they took their leave of the Texan and his daughter. Tara McClendon had attributed to a good deal of her angst. The woman had no compunction about flirting with Miguel in front of her.

Unwanted jealousy continued to fester as Miguel handed her into his waiting sportscar under the watchful eye of the paparazzi. Her thoughts had froze on what had occupied Miguel's time during the past seven months—his business deal with McClendon.

Or more precisely, his relationship with Tara.

Allegra doubted it was coincidence that Miguel had suddenly moved out of their bedroom the same month he'd embarked on a business deal with McClendon. He'd claimed he'd done so out of concern for her during her difficult eighth month, but after meeting Tara, that excuse seemed too convenient.

The American desired Miguel and had commanded the past seven months of his attention. Had they become lovers as well as business associates?

Allegra bristled with jealousy and anger. How dare he accuse her of taking a lover when he was spending the bulk of his time with Tara McClendon!

"Is something bothering you?" he asked as they sped down the avenue.

"Nothing at all."

She wasn't about to give him the satisfaction of knowing she was jealous. For what did that say about her feelings for Miguel?

She shifted uneasily on the plush seat, afraid she knew. She still loved the man who'd broken her heart. The closure she'd sought wouldn't be quick, or painless.

A rainbow of lights from the resorts, hotels and nightclubs reflected off the water, turning the Playa del Carmen shoreline into a lively prism. It was a carnival atmosphere that never changed. Though it was pretty to look at, she found the hustle and bustle of the resort life too cloying.

Had Miguel truly tired of competing with the other moguls along the Maya Riviera? What was the lure of acquiring defunct plantations?

Her fingernails dug into her palms again. Why hadn't he ever discussed his business dealings with her? Why hadn't she pressed him to understand his world?

"I wasn't aware you'd gotten so deeply involved in rural real estate," she said.

"It was a natural transition."

"How so?" she asked. "Why are you so keen on acquiring the haciendas?"

He shot her a quizzical glance before turning his attention back on the road. "They are three of the oldest plantations in the state of Yucatán."

"They have historical significance then," she said over the salsa beat dancing on the wind, holding back her surprise that he'd discuss even this small bit of his business with her.

"*Sí*, the value to me is two-fold."

"How so?" she asked as he smoothly maneuvered the sports car through traffic.

He accelerated, passing cars with ease and proving he was a man clearly in control. "Why the sudden interest in my holdings, *querida*?"

"I've always been interested in what you do, but you never volunteered to discuss your world," she said. "When we were alone, you either seemed too exhausted to engage in a chat, or we spent the time in bed."

He shrugged. "You never complained."

"I should have," she said.

The only sounds were the waves crashing against the shore. She heaved a frustrated sigh, certain he'd shut her out again.

"Fine, I will tell you. For the past year I have been acquiring and restoring henequen plantations to their former glory," he said. "I have converted the larger ones into luxury hotels, and the smaller ones into private resorts."

"I gathered that McClendon owned three plantations," she said in an attempt to keep the conversation moving, scarcely believing he was actually sharing a small part of his world with her.

"*Sí*, but he wouldn't sell them outright."

"Did he have plans for them?" she asked, interested beyond measure.

His fingers tightened around the steering wheel. "No. They were tax write-offs for him, and he was content to let them crumble into dust. Two of them were already in deplorable condition. Time was of the essence to save them."

The passion in his voice caught her by surprise, for the only time she'd seen that intense emotion from him was during sex. To think that he cared this deeply about his culture showed a side of him she hadn't known existed.

"What changed his mind about selling them?" she asked, intrigued by his restoration project.

"Tara McClendon," he said, and she grimaced at the twinge of jealousy her name evoked. "Though she held no interest in restoring henequen plantations, she saw the potential in owning luxury hotels on Riviera Maya."

"They were your bargaining chip."

"*Sí*. It still took an inordinate amount of time to finalize the deal."

"Six or seven months," she said.

A curt nod was her answer.

Allegra cut a glance to the sea that danced with whitecaps, as if it shared her anger over the obvious. Her marriage had taken a sudden downward shift the month before the accident—the same month Miguel struck up this deal with the McClendons.

Her mind spun with images of Tara tonight—the overt flirtations, the meaningful glances, the casual to the point of intimate way she seemed around him.

Yes, their fathers had been friends, but there was more here that roused her darkest suspicions. There was a closeness between them that spoke of an intimacy.

"Is Tara McClendon your lover?" she asked.

"Why do you care?" he shot back.

A good question and one she damn well wasn't about to answer. "How telling that you'd evade the question. Let me rephrase it. Are you and Tara still lovers?"

He muttered a dark curse and stared out the windshield, clearly annoyed she'd pressed him for an answer. It must be one he didn't care to give, for the muscles in his bare forearms rippled and bunched, and his jaw clenched as if in protest of offering a response.

Her stomach crinkled with dread long before he said, "No."

But they had been. He'd mixed business and pleasure with his mistress. He'd shared his exciting world with Tara instead of with his wife.

"She wants you," she said, not about to let him know how badly he'd just hurt her.

"I learn from my mistakes, *querida*. I don't repeat them."

In the wee hours of the morning, Miguel sprawled on the bed in the master bedroom. Despite the welcoming cool breeze that caressed his naked body, he was unable to sleep.

Two scenes kept replaying in his mind. Her obvious terror in the car that she insisted was a flashback of memory. Her earlier claim that she'd been hospitalized the past five months.

The memory loss could be the result of her hitting her head on impact. A severe injury would have required hospitalization. At the least, she may have needed therapy in an effort to regain her memory.

But if any of that were true, then why hadn't his *madre* mentioned it? Why hadn't her uncle told him her mind had blocked the accident when he'd followed her to England? Why hadn't he been informed that his wife had been hospitalized for the past five months?

Because they were lies. She hadn't been injured. She'd ran off with Amando. She'd known exactly what she'd been doing then and now.

He pushed from the bed and prowled to the patio doors, too restless to attempt sleep. The tempest was bearing down on the Yucatán with the same ferocity as generations of conquistadors before him, unyielding and uncompromising, devoid of any compassion.

It would make landfall without conscience and decimate anything that stood in its way.

Miguel didn't believe this part of the peninsula would take a direct hit as it had in previous hurricanes, but the destruction would still be widespread.

Evacuation was imminent. The main highways would be congested with those heading inland in search of lodging. Shelters would be crammed with those who'd stayed, out of choice or necessity.

As before, he'd return to his family's hacienda. Only this time he'd have Allegra with him.

Sí, he'd have Bartholomew Fields investigated and prove she'd never been a patient there. He'd confront her with the

proof of her infidelity and her artful lies. He'd have the satisfaction of watching her squirm before he cast her out of his
life forever.

This time when she left him, it would be in disgrace.

The wind whipped his hair and ribboned over his tense
body as he crossed the *palapa.* He planted both hands on the
low railing and he tipped his head back, bending into the wind.

A flap of white rippled on the terrace above him. Allegra.
He knew it was her without looking.

In the early days of their affair, they'd made love right here
on nights such as this with the moon watching. Even after
they'd married, the charged atmosphere of a storm heightened
their own desires.

His hands tightened on the rail as his body quickened.
Was she aware he was down here, longing for her? Was she
tempting him to take her now?

He bounded up the stairs and stepped onto the terrace, determined to find out her game. Instead of scampering back
into her room, she stood at the upper railing.

The wind plastered her white gown to her body and tore
at her hair. Her head was turned so the moonlight illuminated
her features, and the longing he saw there called to him.

They'd shared this sexual connection from the start. But
during the last trimester of her pregnancy, they'd had to refrain
out of concern for her health.

That's when she'd badgered him to be included in his
business ventures. He'd made that mistake before with Tara
long ago, and he'd vowed never to mix his corporate world
with a lover again—even if that lover was his wife.

That's when they'd lost touch. Now this thing between
them called to him, as fierce as the incoming storm.

He crossed to her in half a dozen strides, his gaze locked on
hers and his body pounding with need. She was his wife. *His!*

"I want you," he said in a voice that had grown gruff with need.

Her chin came up in a show of defiance that caught him off guard. "You had me once, but you cast me aside for an affair with Tara McClendon."

Where the hell did she get that idea?

He sat on the chaise and planted both hands on the curved arms when he ached to pull her to him. "You are jealous."

"No, I'm angry that you hold to this double-standard," she said. "You accuse me of being unfaithful when you were doing the same thing."

"I never broke my vows, *querida*." At least not the vow of fidelity. "Tara and I had an affair five years ago."

He brushed back the hair blowing around her face and cupped her jaw. Her eyelids drifted shut as she leaned into his palm.

A sigh whispered from her and danced along his nerves.

She was getting to him again. Had gotten to him, for he opened his mouth but no sound emerged. Words deserted him completely when she opened her eyes and their gazes collided once again.

Raw need flowed from her and rolled into him with the force of the tide crashing to shore. He tried to rein in the desire racing through him.

Her fingers traced his jaw, his strong chin, the hard bow of his mouth, and he was lost. How many nights had he dreamed of coming to her like this?

His mouth came down on hers with fierce hunger. Her lips soft, her resistance palpable. But only for a charged moment.

She opened to him with a ragged moan. Or was that him voicing his need?

He didn't know. Didn't care. Didn't want anything but this woman. To sink into her and hold tight. To brand her as his again.

Their mouths met in a fusion of fiery need. His hands tore

at her gown, eager, as clumsy as that first night he'd met her on the beach. He'd wanted her with a ferocious hunger then.

He still did.

He walked her backward to the wicker chaise and eased her onto the cushions. Her fingers glided over his chest and torso, stoking a fire in him that threatened to rage out of control.

He burned for her as he had from the start, and he vowed she'd feel the same flames that had consumed them then. He slid fingers that quaked up her bare legs that trembled apart at his touch, his thumbs tracing an invisible line from the bend in her knees to her sex. He memorized the velvet texture of her skin. He drew the spicy-sweet scent that was uniquely her into his lungs, an aphrodisiac he didn't need with her.

She gasped when he stroked the heat of her, her legs closing a fraction only to open wide. Her hips lifted in invitation and her hands clutched at him, pulling him closer.

He whisked the gown from her pale, luminous body and settled into that niche that was made for him. His mouth found hers, the kiss urgent, deep, devouring rational thought. Tongues dueled, hands grasped and tugged with wild urgency.

A clap of thunder shook the *casa*. He went still, gauging the storm—gauging his mood. Both loomed dark.

He rocked back on his haunches, breathing hard, his body screaming for release. He looked down at Allegra. Truly looked at her as his mind absorbed what he was poised to do.

His jaw tensed, his mind railing at his own stupidity in throwing caution to the wind.

"You are on the Pill," he said, his voice breaking the sudden silence that pulsed in the room.

She frowned, her eyes still drowsy with desire. "No."

"No," he repeated, desire switching to annoyance. "You are using some other method of birth control then?"

"No, nothing," she said.

¡Dios mio! This couldn't be happening again. He couldn't be this stupid to let this same woman entrap him in her spell.

"Why the hell not?"

"Because there was no need to take preventative measures when I wasn't sexually active," she said. "Because for six months, I was confined to a hospital."

Again the lies! She'd enticed him up here, and turned the tables on him.

Sí, she knew he'd not take the risk of her becoming pregnant again. She knew he'd not be prepared to protect himself in the middle of the night!

He slid her a cold look, refusing to admire the flush that stole over her small, firm breasts, the heat of her that drew him closer. "Do you think me a fool?"

"I *know* you're an arrogant, stubborn man who refuses to believe he failed to protect his wife," she said, squarely hitting the nail on the head so hard he flinched. "You want to punish me with sex? Go on. Take me. I don't care."

Miguel spat a curse and pressed her down into the cushion, their faces inches apart, their breaths mingling in the charged air. "You'd better care, *querida,* for if I had not stopped, we could have created an innocent life again."

He heard her breath catch. Felt her body stiffen in clear revulsion of that possibility.

He rolled off her and stormed toward the stairs, not looking back, having no more to say to her now. For what did a man say when he'd nearly fallen into the honey trap set by the woman he'd set out to ruin?

CHAPTER FIVE

A BABY? The possibility of her conceiving was so slim it was nearly impossible. It was the unattainable dream that would haunt her the rest of her life. What was it her surgeon had told her?

More surgery might—*might*—repair the damage done in the accident. But with the loss of an ovary, it was doubtful she'd ever get pregnant again.

No, she wasn't worried they could create new life if they'd made love without protection. Her apprehension centered on something far more unsettling.

Miguel believed she'd carried on an affair with Amando Riveras. Nothing could be further from the truth!

With Amando's help, she'd carried on work that Miguel had started and entrusted to his guard. She'd finally been a part of his world and felt a connection to her husband that went beyond sex.

She'd been about ready to surprise Miguel with the wonderful work she'd done with Amando's help. So why hadn't she told him?

She rubbed her forehead, trying to see through the clouds covering so much of her memory. Something had gone terribly wrong. Something that terrified her. Something that concerned Amando and her.

Miguel believed they'd been lovers. He believed the worst in her and wanted to punish her, and yet she ached to make love with him again. What did that say about her?

Allegra drew the woven blanket around her naked body and returned to the bedroom, her body humming with a vibrancy she hadn't felt in months. She couldn't believe being in Miguel's arms again would make her feel so gloriously alive.

Or so sad.

She shut the door and leaned against it, her eyelids drifting closed on a moan borne of self-disgust.

She should have resisted him. She should have at least voiced a protest. But she'd done neither, preferring to believe that his affair with Tara was history.

She'd opened her arms to the man who'd broken her heart. Who'd cast her aside when she needed him the most. She'd lost her daughter, her memory and her husband.

How could she have set aside her own animosity and hurt to satisfy her lust? Satisfy?

Far from it. Kissing Miguel, caressing his magnificent body and having his hands touch her was merely a sip of a vintage wine one only dared to indulge in on rare occasions.

She wanted to get drunk on love again. She wanted what she'd lost.

But she couldn't get it all back. She could give Miguel her heart and body, but she couldn't even give him what he wanted—another child.

And he wanted children. She'd seen the longing in his eyes when the little girl ran into the room at El Trópico.

No, all she could have with him was sex.

They could postpone a divorce and explore the fiery

passions that had ensnared them when they first met. It could last a week, a month, maybe a year.

But in time he'd want another child, and she couldn't give him that.

Her fingers fisted so hard the nails scored her palms.

Cristobel had been the tie to bind them.

She had nothing to hold him now. Nothing but her love.

It hadn't been enough before.

They'd had a wonderful sex life. But he'd shut her out of his world.

She couldn't put herself through that torment. But she admitted she couldn't just walk away from him, either.

A solid, steady pounding jarred Allegra from sleep. What in the world would anyone be building this time of morning?

She crawled from the bed and crossed to the window, momentarily confused by the surreal light. A dark band of clouds clung to the horizon, looking no more than a sooty smudge on a gorgeous seascape.

But she recognized it for what it was. A tropical storm was churning across the Caribbean, and instead of veering away from the Yucatán as had been predicted, it appeared to be heading for them.

The hammering made sense now. Preparations were being made for the worst at the beach house. Miguel must have seen to it early as he'd always done.

Like everyone else on the peninsula, they'd have to evacuate. She dressed quickly in tan slacks and a mint top. Packing was easily done, as she'd never unpacked upon arriving.

She hurried downstairs, certain Miguel would want to leave soon. The uncertainty of what would happen now kept her on edge. She couldn't stay here, and after that nasty scene last night she wasn't sure he'd want to continue with his revenge.

The sheets of wood over the windows rendered the *sala* as dark and oppressive as the charged atmosphere. They'd gone through this together in the early months of their affair.

He'd taken her home and his mother guessed what Allegra only suspected at that point. That she was two months pregnant.

His mother hadn't hidden her displeasure over Allegra "trapping" a rich husband, even though she'd willingly signed a prenuptial agreement. The regal woman had never liked her, and had resented her living in her *casa*.

Allegra shook off that unpleasant memory as she entered the kitchen. Miguel stood with his back to her, hands braced on the counter and spine rigid. A weather forecaster spoke sonorously from a radio on the counter.

The tropical storm had changed course and intensity overnight. An orange alert had been issued for Ione, the feminine name attributed to the hurricane. Winds would be in excess of one hundred fifty miles per hour.

"When is it predicted to make landfall?" she asked, her voice oddly calm despite the danger mushrooming around her.

He straightened, his muscles tensing beneath his fine cotton shirt as if unaware of her approach. "Late today. The evacuation has begun. We will leave within the hour."

"And go where?" she asked, though she feared she knew.

"Hacienda Primaro."

The palatial Gutierrez stronghold since the time his forebears had conquered this land and the people. The place Allegra had fled six months ago with their daughter. But why?

All she recalled of that day were slivered scenes that flashed in her mind like an old movie reel. If her doctor was correct, returning to the *casa* could jar free her memory.

It had certainly worked with Miguel. For being in his arms and feeling his incredible passion confirmed one thing—she wasn't ready to let him go from her life.

"Will you tell your mother why we are together again?" she asked, dreading their confrontation.

His features tensed, hard as the onyx buried deep in the Mexican caverns. "No. You are my wife. That is enough explanation."

Though her memory of leaving the hacienda that day was sketchy, she'd never forgotten how coldly Quintilla had treated her after Cristobel was born.

Miguel crossed his arms, the muscles straining under his crisp white shirt. "She holds you responsible for Cristobel's death."

Like mother, like son?

The thought of living in a villa with Miguel's mother left her nerves twitching.

"Perhaps I should stay in Merida—"

"No. You will come with me."

Unease churned in her belly and danced along her nerves. For all her talk of finding closure, she dreaded returning to the *casa*.

She was terrified of visiting the cemetery. Yes, she knew she needed to cry over her baby's grave, for that may be the key to unlocking more of her memory. But she was unprepared for the depth of emotions that may unleash.

She could only hope when it was over that she'd no longer hear her baby cry out in the middle of the night. Maybe after she went through this hell of grief, she could go on with her life.

"Do you think of her?" she asked.

To her surprise, a shadow of grief passed over his features. "*Sí*, but I don't dwell on what I can't change."

No, he never had. Miguel made decisions and acted on them. He went after what he wanted in life—he conquered his opponents with rapier finesse and rid himself of problems just as easily.

Yet he hadn't disposed of the wife he believed was unfaithful. The wife he blamed for his daughter's death.

"Why didn't you divorce me right after I left?" she asked.

"That would have been too easy for you."

His meaning wasn't lost on her. He'd wanted his pound of flesh—to make her suffer for something she hadn't done.

She chafed her suddenly chilled arms, overwhelmed with thoughts of closure and grief and divorce.

"I'll get your bags," he said. "The sooner we leave, the quicker we'll be out of harm's way."

She didn't believe that for a second. Yes, by tonight she'd be back at the *casa*, removed from the hurricane's fury. But safe?

Not there. Not knowing she'd never been welcomed into his family. Not returning as Miguel's wife in all ways.

For if she lost her heart to her proud conquistador again, she'd be far from safe.

Miguel groused over the increase of vehicles on the *autopista* from Cancún to Merida, adding at least sixty minutes to the normal three-hour drive. He was accustomed to driving alone and in silence, but the quiet that roared between him and Allegra clawed gouges in his patience.

She had been brooding about something since they left. She'd picked at her fingers so intently it was a wonder she hadn't drawn blood.

He'd nearly asked her what the hell was bothering her when they passed through the tollbooth at Caseta X-Can, but he suspected he knew. She was getting cold feet about returning to their home as his wife.

"It is not like you to be so quiet," he said to Allegra when they waited to get through the *Aduana* checkpoint.

"I didn't think you'd appreciate idle chatter," she said.

He smiled, for their conversations in the early days of their relationship had been anything but redundant talk. Another thing he'd enjoyed about her—until they married and she expressed a desire to work.

"You used to have an interest in causes," he said.

"I still do, though that has changed," she said, seeming to perk up a bit. "I'm quite impressed with the work done through *Médecins sans Frontiéres.*"

"Doctors without borders. They have done much work among the Mayan," he said, though he refrained from admitting his own participation.

Secrecy about that organization saved lives, and Allegra had lost what trust he'd had in her six months ago.

"So I've read. I'm quite interested in the mercy mission into Guatemala scheduled for February." Her voice nearly bubbled with excitement.

"You are donating funds to them."

"Actually I'll donate my time and my back if they'll have me," she said, and seemed pleased by the chance to risk her life in the jungle.

"No!"

Silence exploded between them in a cloud so thick he could have struck a line in it. He likely bruised her feelings by putting his foot down so forcefully, but he couldn't let her—

"What do you mean, no?" she asked.

"No is no. It doesn't need an explanation."

"You have no right to tell me what I can and can't do."

"I have every right!" He got a white-knuckled grip on the steering wheel, finding it impossible to concentrate on the traffic snarl at the tollbooth when his English rose was considering something foolhardy. "I am your husband."

She made a very unladylike snort of disagreement. "Now when it suits you," she said, her voice dripping with sarcasm. "We will be divorced by the time the next mission begins."

He swore under his breath at that truth and tossed a wad of bills at the toll keeper at *Caseta Piste*, anxious to vent his frustrations on the open road. But he dragged forth a smile when he recognized the boy in the tollbooth.

"How is your family, Roberto?" he asked.

"Very well," the boy said. "Thank you for helping me get this job, Señor Gutierrez."

"It was nothing."

"It was everything," the boy said. *"Gracias!"*

He nodded in answer and sped off toward Merida, but the pleasure he usually felt about paving the way for a Mayan to better himself was absent. He was not about to allow Allegra to trek off on a dangerous mercy mission.

His word held sway in those circles. He'd make sure her name wasn't on the list of volunteers.

Sí, if she wanted to risk her life, she'd have to do so elsewhere.

His anger cooled with that decision made. But he wondered why he cared so much.

He zipped through the crossroad of the Merida Libre highway, anxious to be home. The route paralleled the *carretera de costa* in a meandering course and had at least one hundred *topes* near the villages to alert drivers to slow down. But it was the only free road and attracted those without pesos, or those with time to spare.

At one time it was his and Allegra's favorite highway to take from the hacienda to the beach house. She'd been hungry to learn of his Mayan heritage, and he'd been proud to teach her.

On that last trip, she'd insisted they buy a *tricicletas* once she gave birth and take their baby on a tour of the old villages in the three-wheeled vehicles. She'd teased him that he should do all the pedaling!

He'd actually considered taking a break from his grueling workload. How easily she'd beguiled him!

"You are too quiet," he said.

"I'm thinking."

To him she appeared to be brooding.

"Do you remember where this road up ahead leads?" he asked, and then before she could voice a lie, he answered for her. "Izmal. I took you there for a horse drawn carriage ride. We saw the Mayan lights and ate—"

"I remember." But again she failed to elaborate.

His fingers tightened on the leather steering wheel as he cut her a quick perusal. Her hands were clenched tightly in her lap. Her face was leached of color again.

"I had thought it was a romantic getaway," he said, annoyed with himself for bringing it up and angry with her for seeming uninterested.

"It was," she said, staring at the lane that curved to merge into the Merida Libre. "I intended to take the *Curoto* that night."

He inhaled sharply, realizing she meant six months ago.

"Why didn't you?"

She shook her head. "I—I don't know."

¡Dios mio! Again with the convenient excuse of memory loss. Did grief and guilt needle her conscience? Did she feel the same pain and loss that tormented him?

She didn't volunteer and he refused to ask. For though their child died because of her carelessness behind the wheel, he blamed himself in part for her death, too.

If he'd been home, Allegra wouldn't have left him with their child. If he'd been a more attentive husband, she wouldn't have sought pleasure in another man's arms.

That cold fact nagged at Miguel as he whipped down the *periferico* that encircled Merida and headed south. Even before he reached the outskirts of the jungle, the sky had darkened to a threatening twilight and the winds increased to make the palms lining the beltway bow and sway.

Though the storm was moving in faster than expected, he found himself more aware of how Allegra's breath trembled. She looked pale and small huddled on the seat beside him.

Whatever pique she'd felt toward him earlier had dissolved after they'd passed the accident site. He felt her intense grief as well as he felt his own, but even if he could think of words to comfort her, he didn't trust his own voice.

So he drove on in tense silence and heaved a relieved sigh when he pulled up to the elaborate Moorish gates that closed off Hacienda Primaro from the world. Still, the only sound in the car was the whir of his window lowering and her quick breaths.

He jabbed in the code on the keypad and waited for the gates to swing open, his blood pulsing to a ruthless tempo. Once the gates rattled open in defiance of the wind, he shot up the winding lane toward the hacienda toward the garage artfully built to complement the historic hacienda.

Miguel jetted into his slot, killed the engine and leaped from the car.

"¡Hola!" A wiry young boy of ten burst into the garage. "It is good you are home, Señor Gutierrez. Señora was worried."

He reached out and ruffed the boy's thick black hair, gaining a broad smile for his effort. "She worries overmuch."

The boy bobbed his head. "Sí. It is the way with women," the boy said, and Miguel bit back a smile at the boy's astuteness.

His *madre* was always fretting over something—usually the fact that he'd refused to divorce and marry again. He knew she wouldn't appreciate the fact he'd brought his wife back home—in that Allegra was correct.

Miguel walked to the rear of the SUV just as Allegra opened the passenger door. The boy, who'd been shadowing him, peeked around the back of the car.

The boy's mouth dropped open. "Señora Vandohrn? Is it really you?"

"Yes, Juan," she said. "My, look how you've grown."

"*Sí,* I am fourteen years now," Juan said, puffing his scrawny chest out. "The man of the house, my *madre* says."

"Your mother is lucky to have you," Allegra said, and there was no mistaking the sad tone that crept into her voice.

"*Gracias!*" Juan glanced at Miguel as if unsure how to proceed with the former lady of the house.

Miguel hefted a wheeled pilot case from his SUV. "Take *señora*'s baggage to the master suite."

"*Sí, señor.*" Juan latched on to the case and flashed a wide smile at Allegra whose face now glowed with color. "It is good you are home, *señora.*"

Her smile stretched tight. "Thank you, Juan."

No sooner had the boy disappeared into the house when Allegra rounded on him. "There is bound to be talk about why I've returned after six months."

"I care nothing about gossip."

"I do," she said. "So will your mother."

Her voice had risen on the last two words, carrying an annoyed note that scraped bloody gouges along his nerves. "You are my wife. There is no need for explanations on why you are here with me."

"God forbid if word got out that I was forced to come here," she said, chin raised.

He yanked his carry-on from the SUV and slammed the door so hard she flinched. "As I recall you welcomed me with open arms last night on the terrace."

A deeper crimson flooded her cheeks. "I didn't invite you above stairs."

¡Bravo! She'd gouged him again, like a bull would gore a careless matador. And he had been careless with her!

He gave a sharp nod to admit as much and pointed to the door that opened onto the portico. "You know the way. Let's get inside before the storm hits."

He cynically wondered which storm would cause more destruction. The one that battered the peninsula, or the tempest that would descend on his family.

CHAPTER SIX

ALLEGRA turned on legs that wobbled, dreading each step that took her closer to the house. She'd loved this historic hacienda when she'd first laid eyes on it, but her first few days living here as Miguel's bride convinced her she was nothing more than a visitor. An unwelcome one in her mother-in-law's hostile eyes.

But Miguel never noticed, and when she brought it to his attention, he confronted his mother who swore Allegra had misunderstood.

After all, a pregnancy rendered a woman supersensitive to everything. That was the end of it.

Or was it?

Her head hurt from the stress of coming here. Trying to dredge up old memories would only make it worse.

Quintilla Barrosa y Gutierrez stepped in front of Allegra. "You dare to come back here?"

As usual, the woman didn't attempt to hide her animosity.

"I have every right to visit my daughter's grave," Allegra said.

"You should have done so before now," Señora Barrosa said, flushing as Miguel strode into the foyer.

"What is this?" Miguel's dark eyes narrowed.

"After what she did, how could you bring her here?" his mother asked.

"She is *mi esposa*."

His mother released a snort of disbelief. "If you have brought her here to stay, then I will leave."

"You will stay here at the hacienda until the danger of the storm has passed. *¿Queda claro?*"

Challenge flared in her dark eyes, but she gave a curt nod. "Very well. For you I will tolerate her for this short visit."

With a lift of her chin, his mother marched off toward the *sala*. Her heels clicked an angry staccato on the terra cotta tiles.

"She's right, you know," Allegra said. "You shouldn't have brought me here."

"I disagree. You want closure? Then look for it here where you chose to end our marriage."

If only she could. "I'll be in my room," she said, and started up the stairs, desperate for rest, for time alone to sort this out in her mind.

"Our room," he said to her back, but she continued walking up the wide stairs as if she didn't hear him.

As if she could voice a reply after that arrogant statement! Her body hummed at the thought of sharing a room with Miguel.

Last night had been another wondrous reminder of what they'd had together. She hadn't realized how starved she was for his touch, his kiss, his possession.

But the second he'd embraced her and branded her with his kiss, she'd gone up in flames of desire. The burn still lingered, a hell she'd endured on the drive up for all she'd had to do was reach over and touch him as she'd longed to do. All she had to do was beg him to finish what he'd started.

He'd take her again, she thought as she stepped into the master suite. Though the bed was enormous, it looked cozy in this glorious room dressed in rich reds and gold. Even in the semidark of a storm-cloaked dusk, the suite quivered with a vibrancy that left her trembling.

She crossed to the window, her steps in tempo with the distant rumbling thunder. The storm would hit soon, an hour at the most. But until it did, the garden was bathed in a surreal glow. More vivid and sensual than the priceless paintings that were displayed in the Gutierrez private gallery.

Her gaze drifted across the clipped lawn and paused at the aged bathhouse before moving on to the Mayan hut authentically restored and protected.

In this Miguel excelled, for he'd done all in his power to protect the ancient heritage that his ancestors had nearly stamped out when they came here to conquer this new world. If he'd just been able to shore up and protect his marriage as well.

She shook her head as the distant henequen-processing chimney peeked above a lush wall of shrubs. Sisal, the green gold of Mexico, tripled the Gutierrez family wealth. But it was Miguel who became the first billionaire.

She looked away, only to have the Moorish facade of the chapel loom into view. It ceased serving as the religious home to the family and workers when the sisal empire fell.

But as all his family before him, she and Miguel were married there. All his ancestors were buried in the cemetery. Their daughter as well?

She stood at the window a moment longer, trembling inside with the awful emptiness of loss. The wind whined through the eaves, sounding like a child's whimper. *Her child.*

With a curse, she rushed from the room and took the back stairs to the kitchen. Thunder rumbled a warning as she burst outside and ran the length of the portico.

The wind whipped her hair and shoved at her, as if trying to push her back into the house.

Allegra would have none of it. She'd been denied visiting her daughter's grave. She'd gladly steal this moment before the storm drove her back to the house and shelter. Back to Miguel and his dark suspicions and darker passions.

She ran across the lush lawn toward the Moorish keyhole opening carefully cut into the acacia hedge. An adobe wall painted lavender-blue stretched toward the chapel facade where a bell still hung in the uppermost arched belfry.

An iron gate fashioned in the same old world Moorish charm closed off the cemetery. She fought open the catch, then pushed with all her might to open the gate enough to slip inside.

The wind ripped it from her grasp and banged it shut with a resounding clack of metal. The sound vibrated through her, but a deeper tremor threatened to bring her to her knees.

She stared at the headstones rising like sentries over the dead. Lichen clung to the majority of old ones.

One brighter marble stone stood out from the other. A seraphim with wings arched gazed serenely heavenward, as if beseeching God to protect the precious life entombed within.

"Cristobel," she whispered, the name stolen away by the wind.

Her breath caught, her heart hammering so hard she was dizzy. This was what nine months of waiting and excited devotion came down to. Standing over the grave of her child. Knowing it was her fault that this life had been taken, knowing that no matter what she did she'd never be able to change what happened that fateful night.

Lightning struck in the jungle and lit the sky overhead, the thunder booming a nanosecond later as if in agreement. A part of her recognized the danger in staying here, but the wounded part of her didn't care.

She'd lost what mattered most to her. There was simply nothing left to lose.

Allegra crossed the thick carpet of clipped grass to the grave and knelt.

Cristobel Yolande Maneula Vandohrn y Gutterierz
Beloved daughter of Allegra Vandohrn and
Miguel Hernando Barrosa de Gutierrez

The words blurred before her eyes, the finality of this slicing into her heart with brutal force. She'd had her daughter one month—one month.

It was still so hard to believe any of this had happened. Cristobel's death. Her surgeries and memory loss. Miguel's estrangement.

A clap of thunder gave her headache new energy. She swiped the tears from her eyes and read the rest of the inscription aloud.

"A treasure beyond worth." Her voice caught on the last.

It was apt, for nothing on this earth would ever come close to meaning more to her than her daughter. Coming here didn't change anything.

Closure would take time, for this was all new to her. She couldn't just drop by once and expect to feel vindicated. She'd need time to put this part of her life behind her and move on. Time was the one thing she was in short supply of.

Lightning arrowed to the ground again and thunder boomed in its wake. The ground trembled just as the first fat raindrops splattered the marble.

She reached a trembling hand out and traced the droplets over the cold stone, desperate to feel a connection to her daughter again, but feeling nothing but hard marble.

It wasn't right because at times she could hear her daughter's last pained cries, still recognize the terror in that baby's voice. Had she suffered? She wished she knew, for the torment of thinking the worse robbed her of sleep, of peace, of believing she'd ever grant herself the smallest forgiveness.

Her fingers curled, the nails scraping over the cold marble.

A sob caught in her throat, another following close behind. She bent her head and hugged her middle, aching so badly she wanted to die.

"I'm so sorry," she said, over and over until she could no longer form words, until nothing escaped her but agonized whispers that echoed in her heart.

No, there'd be no closure here. She didn't want to forget what had happened.

She wanted to remember the fiery love she'd shared with Miguel. The love that had swelled her heart when she'd held her baby girl in her arms. The love that had promised forever, yet ended far too soon.

A masculine shoulder brushed hers, and energy skittered over her skin like an electrical charge. "You shouldn't be here," Miguel said, kneeling beside her, his voice a fathomless depth of emotion she'd never heard before.

She looked at him and her heart squeezed painfully. His handsome face was deadly somber, the dark, mesmerizing eyes sheened with moisture and mirroring a grief that rivaled her own.

She'd never believed this strong man capable of tears, yet the evidence was right before her. That vulnerability speared her heart and sank into her soul, leaving her trembling to reach out to him. To comfort him. To share their loss.

"I don't know how to say goodbye to her," she said.

He was silent a long time. "The Mayan believe the dead ascend into a higher being," he said. "Cristobel is in the stage of purification, but she hears us, sees us."

"Do you believe that?"

He shrugged, and his handsome face gave nothing away of his feelings. "I believe she is at peace."

Which was more than she could say for them.

"Come. You can talk with her another time. The storm is nearly upon us," he said.

He was wrong, for the storm had raged within them both for six months. It was anyone's guess if they'd come out of this unscathed, or if this fragile bond would be forever shattered.

Miguel shoved the crippling sense of loss to the far reaches of his mind. Coming here alone was one thing. Coming here with Allegra laid bare emotions he refused to let her see.

The wind gusted and tore at the trees, shredding leaves in a green shower. But it wasn't until a *lamina* tore off the roof of a shed and catapulted over the old henequen factory that he realized the storm was far stronger than expected.

He grabbed Allegra's hand. "We must seek shelter now."

She kept up with him as they ran across the lawn. They were nowhere near the house when the sky opened up and the cold, hard rain pelted them.

He could barely stand up against the wind and hold on to Allegra. With effort he pulled her into the private bathhouse behind the villa. The door slammed shut behind them, and he bolted it so it wouldn't blow open and rip off the hinges.

A bolt of lightning lit up the interior through the clerestory windows, reflecting off the blue mosaic tiles like strikes of cobalt fire. Even the water in the pool glimmered with a surreal light.

A deception, for danger danced around them with every labored breath, each nervous glance. They could end up here for hours.

Alone.

¡Maldita sea! He must have gone loco, for why else would he seek sanctuary with a woman who roused something torrid and primal in him. A woman who tormented his sleep six months after she'd deserted him.

A woman he wanted with each breath he drew.

He ached to sink into her again and relive the heat and passion of their early marriage. He wanted his wife back and to hell with revenge, but that was a fool's way and he was no fool.

She'd used him. Now, he'd use her.

"If, as you say, you've been celibate the past six months," he said as he went about lighting old wall sconces, for if the power weren't already out, it would be soon, "your needs must be great."

"Back to that, are we?"

"It is a subject I'm most interested in. Now, when was the last time you made love?"

She stared at him with a detached air that he found arousing, as if she were challenging him to make a move. Good. The chase was on!

"You know when."

His blood stirred at her implication, but he wouldn't be so beguiled. "How could I know when you and Riveras made love? Or have you moved beyond him now?"

"I never let him touch me," she snapped, and then after expelling a deep breath, added, "The last time I made love was with you when I was just eight months pregnant."

And hours afterward, he'd had to rush her to the doctor due to contractions and the fear the baby was coming early. That was the last time he'd made love to her, and the last time he'd slept with her.

He shrugged in reply, for he had no wish to continue lobbing accusations of fidelity or lack thereof back and forth. That was over and done with.

"We could have made it back to the house," she said, and turned away from him to fluff her damp hair, the motion emphasizing her pert breasts.

"It was too dangerous to try."

Yet didn't a far different danger lurk here in the tranquil confines of the bathhouse? A haven for lovers, he'd once called this place when he'd first brought Allegra here.

He'd fallen helplessly under her spell then. She was an enchantress, a pagan goddess who'd danced naked in the moonlight with him. She'd do so again, but this time he'd remain in control!

"So since we are discussing our sexual history," she said as she strolled the perimeter of the pool. "When was the last time you made love?"

Ah, that had the distinct ring of jealousy to it. "I would not know the exact date."

"Take a guess," she said.

He spread his arms wide. "I am not the type man who talks about his conquests with his wife."

"No, you are the type man who doesn't chat about anything with his wife," she said, bitterness ringing in her voice.

"What is there to discuss?"

"The way you've always shut me out of your business life," she said. "Have you always done that with your women?"

He stiffened, resenting that "your women" remark which made him sound like he had a harem at his disposal. "I told you I do not mix business with my personal life."

"Ah, but your life is your business."

He had no comeback for that, for in some ways it was true. Or at least he had been before Cristobel's birth.

He'd known then when he'd looked at his beautiful *niña* that he wanted to spend private time with his family. He wanted to spend time with his wife, but before he could make that drastic change in his life, she ran off.

"I made the mistake of discussing my business plans to my lover," he said, giving her a bit of insight into his reasoning because he was tired of her harping about this desire to talk about anything and everything he did in a day. "I vowed never to do it again."

"Why? Did she trade company secrets or something?"

"*Sí.* She closed on the deal I had been working on." He dropped the louver for a window into place and secured it with two iron hooks, blocking the remnants of light but not the bitter memory of being young and green and trusting of a woman.

"Who was she?" she asked.

He debated all of two seconds whether to tell her. Why the hell not? She'd likely guess it anyway.

"Tara McClendon," he said.

Her mouth dropped open, then shut with a clack of teeth. "She betrayed you, yet you did business with her again?"

He waved a hand to dismiss the matter. "One had nothing to do with the other."

"How can you say that?"

"Because this last deal was strictly business and she is an astute businesswoman." The fact she could not understand that proved she let her emotions rule her.

"Our marriage never stood a chance," she said with a surfeit of sarcasm that scraped along his nerves as she stood in the flickering light like a wraith while thunder rocked the walls surrounding them. "What you didn't dictate about our life together, your mother did. I had no say regarding the house or my own daughter."

His jaw clenched so tight he heard the bones grate. Didn't she realize that she'd been as dominant and demanding as he in the bedroom? That he'd reveled in her aggressive bent with lovemaking? That no woman had ever compared to her?

"The *casa* has been my *madre*'s home for thirty-five years," he said. "It was my home, my heritage. You knew that when we married."

"Yes, a huge hacienda with lots of space." She glared at him, but he caught the sheen of hurt in her eyes. "Yet this was my prison. You even hired a guard to watch me."

Which he'd regret for the rest of his life, but then he'd never suspected his pregnant wife would break her marriage vows. "*¡Maldita sea!* I hired him to protect you because I knew the dangers. I'd lost my brother to kidnappers, and I wasn't about to let you become their next victim."

A tense hum of quiet expanded in the room as she took that in with wide eyes. "Would it have hurt you to tell me that?"

He made a slashing motion with his hand, unwilling to discuss the demons that drove him with her now. "I told you there were those in Mexico who made a living off kidnapping the wealthy. That should have been explanation enough."

"It was, but I'd have understood your reasoning far better if I'd known you'd suffered such a personal tragedy," she said. "But then you never shared your hopes and fears with me."

Nor would he! He'd wanted to weave dreams with her, but he was afraid to let himself love at that depth. He'd held back revealing too much of what was in his heart for fear he'd lose her, and that would destroy him.

"What did you expect of me, *querida*?" he said, slamming the door on those feelings that weakened a man—the ones that tried to gain a foothold now. "A cottage with gardens and a husband who came home every night?"

Her chin came up at that, and he admired the fact she hadn't given in to tears or theatrics even while he hated that she'd drawn him into this dialogue. "Yes, maybe I did."

His English rose was far out of her league, a fact he'd been aware of when he first met her. "You should have used more precaution then, *querida*, for our child tied you to my world and to me."

"Of course, I forgot this was all my fault," she said, her pale cheeks crimson. "I trapped you into marriage by getting pregnant. You, the billionaire with a string of celebrity lovers. The man who seduced me on my own private beach." She marched up to him, fire and hurt and passion glittering in her eyes. "If you didn't wish to create a child, you should have used protection. But then it seems you still expect a woman to take full responsibility."

He grasped her upper arms and pulled her against him, his blood pumping hotter as her hardened nipples pressed against his chest. "Know this, Allegra. I never regretted marrying you or having our daughter. Until you took both from me."

Allegra slammed her fists against the hard wall of his chest, fed up with hearing that she'd been the one to destroy their marriage, their future. But getting this close and touching him was a mistake. She knew that the second energy shot up her limbs and set her on fire.

"You walked away from our marriage two months before Cristobel was born, Miguel. You!"

"Out of concern for your condition," he said, trapping her fists and bringing her even closer to him. "The doctor made it clear that you were to have bed rest or risk losing our *niña*. He emphasized private bed rest."

"So you moved out of the house?"

"I had business that took me away," he said.

"How convenient!"

Heat of an entirely different kind flowed into her, turning her limbs languid, her thoughts muzzy. Her body responded to the intense charge of his despite the provocation he stirred in her. But then this energy that arced between them had been magnetically fierce from the moment she'd met him.

She'd known when they touched that he was the only man for her. That she'd never feel the same intensity of passion or depth of love with any one else. Just Miguel.

"I barely heard from you in three months. You weren't around enough to even know your daughter!"

He muttered a vulgarity. "You are not the only one with regrets, *querida*."

So he hadn't learned to cope with that truth on his own terms yet. "A shame you didn't bother to share that confession with me sooner, but then that would have necessitated you spending more than ten minutes with us." She glared at him. "But then, you'd have had to talk to me."

"We are talking now, and it is solving nothing!"

Allegra shoved away from him, feeling the discordant throb to her soul. "We are arguing, which is better than what we had for most of our marriage."

"We had great sex."

He reached out and grazed a knuckle down her flushed cheek, his touch setting off a firestorm within her that flowed down her body and settled in her womb, making it tremble for something she could never have again.

"It wasn't enough," she said.

She made to shove his hand away, but he caught her wrist in the blink of an eye. Though his restraint was a gentle manacle, his features were as hard and cold as the cobalt tiles they stood on.

"Why did you turn to Amando Riveras after Cristobel was born?" he asked.

Allegra stared at him, disgusted that he still chose to believe she'd been unfaithful. His mind was set.

Well, so was hers. Only she remembered those long, lonely nights spent at this hacienda, waiting for the husband who rarely came home. When he did, he preferred to sleep alone.

She moved in the same tight circle as he, hands clenched and heart thundering. It felt so good to be angry at him. To vent the frustrations that had festered in her for so long.

"For the last time, Amando wasn't my lover," she said.

"Then why did you leave the *casa* every day?" He stared at her, one hard, mean, unforgiving man who looked capable of violence.

Well, she could be hard and unforgiving in this, too, for he'd not only abandoned her, but he'd forsaken a promise to the people he'd promised to help.

"I was helping Amando with the humanitarian work you'd begun and abandoned," she said, letting her pride ring in her voice. "I was making a difference in your world, Miguel."

He yanked her against him, nostrils flared and eyes snapping with fury and some emotion she'd never seen before. "¡*Hostias!* What did you get involved in?"

"What you'd promised to do for the refugees yet abandoned to build a bigger empire for yourself."

"No!"

"Yes!" She shoved him hard and twisted to break free.

He teetered on the edge of the pool, eyes wide, sensual mouth parted. Then with a wicked smile, he yanked her against him and sent them toppling backward into the pool.

CHAPTER SEVEN

BEFORE his back hit the tranquil surface, his mouth fused with hers—hungry, demanding, passionate.

The kiss stole her breath away and breathed life into her just the same. She clung to Miguel and the promise in his kiss, dimly aware of the warm water rushing over them.

He was strong and passionate and hers.

She tore at his shirt, tugging the wet cloth away from the expansive breadth of his chest. Even in the water his skin was warm to the touch. Warm and hard and silk-on-steel smooth.

Her legs tangled with his for a moment, then he pushed them to the surface. He pressed her against the blue-tiled side of the pool and tore his mouth from hers. His breath escaped him in short, angry puffs. The mouth that had ravished her looked so grim she wanted to scream.

Just like that and he could turn off his desire. Not so for her. Her body hummed with restless energy.

"You will not beguile me again," he said, and she wondered if the admonition was for her or him.

"I didn't initiate the kiss."

"*Sí,* you did with your enticing body and mouth that begged to be kissed. But I will not risk another pregnancy."

She stared up at him, trapped by his masculine power and

the raw need coursing through her. Her pride urged her to withhold the truth, but her foolish heart couldn't bear the thought of deceiving him.

"The chances of me getting pregnant are highly remote," she said, the words still painful to admit even after all this time.

His brow closed together over his patrician nose. "How can that be when you admitted you weren't on the Pill or using any means of birth control?"

"The accident," she said simply.

"Explain this to me."

Was he serious? He had to know the details of her injuries, yet the tense cant of his head and that impatient questioning glint in his dark eyes screamed bewilderment.

This hadn't been some frivolity their families had omitted telling him about. They'd kept pertinent details from her husband. And instead of searching for answers himself, he'd taken their word as truth.

"I nearly bled out before reaching the hospital," she said, earning her a darker scowl. "But because it was internal, nobody realized the danger I was in until it was nearly too late."

"Why wasn't I told about this?" He had been so devastated by the loss of his daughter and the news of Allegra's infidelity that he had believed all he had been told about the accident— at the time Allegra's was not a voice to be trusted.

"Ask your mother that question. Uncle Loring told me that she came to the hospital the night of the accident, and again after I'd had surgery."

His dark eyes snapped with anger. "You spoke with her as well?"

"No," she said, the memory of waking alone and terrified was still fresh. "I was unconscious when they brought me in. By the time I awoke, my uncle was the only person attending me."

A ruddy flush streaked across his cheekbones, but that was

the only indication he experienced any guilt for not being there for her. "I want to doubt you are telling the truth, but I sense there is more going on here than I was told."

She went still, absorbing what he was saying. Her pulse sped up and her heart warmed with the first rays of hope.

Miguel had never questioned his *madre's* word.

But it was obvious he was doing so now. He'd been kept in the dark much like Allegra had been, with their families striving to separate lovers when they needed each other the most.

She hated her uncle for his part in this as much as she despised his conniving mother. It was obvious her uncle strove to protect her from the husband who was causing her nothing but heartache.

His mother had never believed Allegra good enough. She'd hated Allegra for trapping Miguel into marriage.

But dwelling on hatred only made it fester.

"I won't forgive you so easily for giving up on us," she said. "But I still want you."

She pressed her palms over his chest and trailed them down into the water, tracing the ridges of his pectorals before venturing lower. The desire he'd carefully banked broke free, blazing in his eyes and quickening his breathing.

He groaned and lifted her from the water, coming up and over her in one powerful surge. His eyes were near black with desire—his body hard against her yielding one.

"This could all be a lie."

"You know it's not, but believe what you will, Miguel," she said. "You always have before."

"Bruja," he growled without animosity. "I am immune to your spell."

"I wish I could say the same about you," she said, for in his arms her will to remain aloof deserted her.

"Then let us burn together again."

Before she could think to answer, his head lowered. His lips grazed hers. Once. Twice.

She quivered, moaned, then lifted her face to his.

For a long moment he didn't move. She was certain he didn't breath, either. God knew she held her breath, wondering if he'd kiss her again.

Would he deny them what they both wanted?

His mouth settled over hers with a groan.

Of surrender? Yes, but surely it was she who capitulated, for her arms slid around his neck and she stopped trying to rationalize. She just gave over to feeling the sensuous power of this man at this moment.

For after all was said and done, she wanted him. She wanted to forget the hell they'd been through and be the lover in his arms once more.

That soft moan of surrender was all it took for Miguel's mind to click off, for the recriminations and warnings to go silent. This need to have her was stronger than the raging tempest, more powerful than sanity.

He wasn't alone in his passion. Her small hands slid down his chest, tracing ribs and sinew and setting off explosions of raw need within him.

He tore off her clothes and his, nearly losing it as their bare flesh came together with sizzling need. Surely they set off sparks.

"You've been working out," she said as she ran her hands over his pectorals.

He'd done no such thing, but he hadn't the patience or inclination to explain the changes in his body. With her hands freely exploring him and sending his libido into overdrive, he was doing good to fish a foil condom packet from his discarded trousers.

He'd thrown himself into work so he'd be too exhausted

to be haunted by the tragedy. Yet even then thoughts of Allegra intruded his sleep.

Now she was in his arms, and the reality was so much sweeter than any dream.

She arched and pulled him close, and he drove into her in one long, smooth thrust. An explosion of heat jetted through him.

The fit was exquisite, the sense of rightness all encompassing. This was the home he'd mourned, the melding of two hearts that called to him in the dead of night.

He pumped into her, taking pleasure in her matching his thrusts, his arousal spurred on by the sexy mewling sounds she made. Her legs clung to his hips while her fingernails raked his back.

This was raw, carnal need. Nothing more.

Each thrust and drugging kiss crackled with erotic frenzy, as if they only had a stolen moment together, as if they couldn't get enough of the other.

And they couldn't.

He could not tell who was more demanding. Him or her.

Time fell away as their desire roared to life. He was taking her with the same fierce need that had gripped him the first time they'd made love. She was welcoming him with the same unbridled passion, clinging to him, bucking with each thrust, sucking him deeper into the silken web of her sensuality.

He wanted to go slow, draw the pleasure out until she begged for release. But it would be easier to order the wind to cease than to dominate this moment.

It was a race and a duel of wills, each pushing the other, each demanding more. He felt her coming and pushed her over the edge of desire, following her over into that tumultuous vortex of satiation, controlling this tiny moment that presented itself.

She dug her fingernails into his buttocks and arched into

him, his name bursting from her trembling lips in a sultry whisper, her body quivering and convulsing around him until he could hold back no longer. One final thrust and he gave in to the primal mating call.

Their gazes locked as they climaxed together, breaths mingling, hearts beating as one. But what he saw in her eyes terrified him, for it was a reflection of his own vulnerability with her.

He could feel the heat of her throb within his soul, giving him life again in a heartbeat, joining him to her through an eternity of need.

His lungs burned as he rolled off her and sprawled on his back, breath sawing deep and ragged. Outside the hurricane roared like a savage beast loosed from hell, but it was tame compared to the emotional storm churning within him.

He'd planned to use her for his pleasure then dump her as punishment for the pain she'd put him through. But he hadn't considered having sex with her would make him feel whole again.

He hated her more for stealing his heart than for the fortune in jewels she'd taken. He hated her for taking Cristobel from him. He hated her for leaving him for another, despite her denial to the contrary.

Yet the image of her offering herself to him was branded on his soul. But it was the ruptured condom that had his fingers curling into tight fists.

He rolled to his feet and shrugged into his trousers. The quiet finally penetrated his anger.

Either the worst of the storm had passed over, or there was a break in the tempest. It couldn't come at a better time.

"How long before you have your next cycle?" he asked.

He heard her rise followed by the rustle of clothes. "It doesn't matter. I can't conceive."

"Fine. Time will tell."

He threw on his shirt and left the front undone, the only thing he could do since half the buttons were missing now. The reminder of how hungry she'd been to seduce him dumped more fuel onto the already smoldering embers of desire.

There was no way he could stay here with her and not touch her again.

"Get dressed," he said as he turned to face her.

But she wasn't there and neither were her clothes. He stormed around the bathhouse, checking everywhere.

"Allegra!"

The slamming of the door was his only answer.

Miguel pushed outside just as the rain commenced anew. The wind picked up speed again. Beneath the portico, he saw her running toward the door.

He tore off after her, his steps slowing once he'd reached the protection of the house as well. Now was not the time to catch her. He needed to purge himself of the conflicting feelings and refocus his energy on what he would do with his wife.

Let her think she escaped him for now. She'd find out before long that he was far from finished with her.

In bed. Or out of it.

Allegra woke with a start, a frantic sensation that made her heart race and her pulse pound. It happened so often she should be used to it by now, but it always unsettled her.

This time it was worse, perhaps because of seeing Cristobel's grave. Perhaps because she'd made love with Miguel again.

She stretched gingerly in the luxurious bed, testing muscles that hadn't been used in months. Her legs, back, between her thighs—all were unusually tender. How rambunctious had she been with Miguel?

Extremely, she recalled with a flush. If only he'd felt it with his heart, but she knew for Miguel sex was nothing more than satisfying an itch. If their vows had meant anything to him, he wouldn't have left her here as a virtual prisoner, dominated by his mother.

He wouldn't have cut her out of his life.

Even so she'd sat in her room until the wee hours, fretting if he'd visit her here. But he hadn't.

She'd served her use to him.

She'd been painfully reminded just how wonderful her sexual life had been with Miguel. And just how hardheaded he was when it came to believing her.

He stubbornly insisted she'd had an affair with Amando Riveras. Nothing could be further from the truth, but he hadn't asked her to explain what she'd been doing. Perhaps he didn't wish to admit that he'd failed the gentle Mayans who were escaping Guatemala.

Perhaps his indomitable pride wouldn't allow him to admit that his English wife had taken over the task to help those less fortunate.

A glance at the clock showed it was half past nine. She hadn't slept that long in months.

Allegra leaped from the bed and darted into the en suite bathroom. Thirty minutes later she emerged refreshed.

She chose a simple pair of jade slacks and charcoal blouse for today and left her room. What would this day hold in store?

As she entered the dining room her mother-in-law set the delicate cup and saucer down with care, though Allegra sensed it was done to draw out the moment and strain Allegra's patience. "You are not welcome here."

Allegra didn't even flinch at the coldly delivered statement. "Where is Miguel?"

She donned a disgusted mien. "He said he must visit

Tumbenkahal and inspect the damage done in the wake of the hurricane."

"When is he expected to return?"

"I do not know. A day. Maybe two."

Señora Barrosa feathered her fingers over the white brocade tablecloth, the movement deceptively serene. But the cold glint in her eyes told the truth. She hated Allegra, and with Miguel gone she would unleash her wrath.

"Miguel told me that you returned to Cancún to sell the beach house," she said.

"Yes." She refused to divulge more to this critical woman.

Her mother-in-law inclined her head in the manner a queen would acknowledge a lesser subject. "I will give you twice the value of it if you agree to leave Mexico now and never return."

Allegra stilled as the same proposal triggered a memory. Like before, it came and went in a puff of smoke. But this time she couldn't shake off the feeling that her mother-in-law had tried to buy her off before.

But since her memory prior to the accident was intact, that meant she'd offered to pay her to leave Miguel right before it happened.

"Well?" Señora Barrosa asked.

She stared at the woman. "Mexico is a big country."

The senora's mouth thinned. "Fine. Agree to stay away from the Yucatán Peninsula and the money is yours."

It would be more than enough to provide a cushion for her as she started life on her own. Miguel would surely be so furious with her for depriving him of his vengeance that he'd divorce her without hesitation.

She'd be free. And alone.

Yet she refused to take the money from her mother-in-law, partly because she was not about to bow to the old harridan's wishes, and partly because she couldn't forget the look in his eyes when he realized he'd been lied to about Allegra's injuries.

"Keep your offer," she told Miguel's mother.

Anger snapped in Señora Barrosa's dark eyes. "You are a fool! There is nothing for you here."

"My daughter is buried in the Hacienda Primaro Cemetery."

The señora tossed her hands in the air and snorted. "You have not bothered to visit once in the past six months. Why drag forth this concern now?"

"I couldn't make the trip before." But she kept the reason to herself.

"You shouldn't have made it now," she said, venom dripping off her words as she got to her feet. "Think about my offer. It is the best you will receive from my family."

That truth would hurt more coming from Miguel. She waited for her mother-in-law to leave before doing the same. With Miguel gone, she wasn't about to stay here a moment longer than she must.

An idea had began forming in her head the second she learned what Miguel was doing. This time she'd follow through on what her heart bid her to do.

The small altar in the alcove to her right caught her attention. She skittered to a stop, overwhelmed with love and grief as she stared at her baby's face.

Cristobel was a beguiling mix of her and Miguel. His dark hair and coloring. Her nubbin nose and blue eyes.

Her arms still ached to cradle her close, kiss her baby's soft face. Her heart broke to know that if she hadn't taken her with her that day, she may still be alive.

Regret was a horrible thing to live with. She'd made so many mistakes in her marriage. Why had she left the *casa* that day?

She'd tried and failed to remember. She was likely going to the beach house, her respite when she was troubled.

A chill feathered up her spine. So why hadn't Amando Riveras accompanied her?

She gave up trying to force the memory and focused on the altar. She'd seen others in the house—one dedicated to Miguel's father—one to his brother who'd died when she was a child. They were tastefully arranged to depict objects that held importance to the deceased in this world.

Cristobel had been too young to form attachments, but there were items that would appeal to a little girl. The porcelain doll like those found in the tourists' shops was dressed in an exquisitely embroidered *huipil* blouse and woven *corte* skirt.

The stuffed bear was one she'd purchased herself, a whimsical creature intended to make her baby smile. Given the animosity between her and Señora Barrosa, it warmed her heart in that it had been included to the altar that was painstakingly designed to reflect a Mayan theme. How odd she hadn't chosen Spanish, but then maybe this was to honor Miguel who'd done tremendous work helping the Mayans.

Allegra thought of the young Mayan couple who'd come here seeking help from Miguel. She'd taken it upon herself to spend long hours teaching them rudimentary English so they'd blend well further north. She hoped that unlike her, they had settled in a new home now.

She'd had no qualms about helping the Mayans then. She certainly had none now.

She returned to her room and changed into jeans, T-shirt and track shoes in less than fifteen minutes. Another two minutes and she was outside standing beneath the portico, twisting her hair up under a ball cap and deciding how to put her plan into motion.

The memory of doing just this countless times washed over her as she left her room. If Miguel had just asked her about her secret meetings then, she'd have told him. But now he didn't believe she was doing good. He had chosen to believe the worst of her and Amando Riveras.

She shivered as she stepped from the *casa,* a cold icy bleat of a memory touching her when she thought of the guard. Perhaps that was triggered by her earlier question of why he hadn't accompanied her when she left the hacienda.

Moments passed before Jorge, the gardener's youngest son, rushed over. "It is good to see you back home, *señora.*"

She smiled, not wanting him to think her return was permanent. "How is your sister and brother-in-law?"

"They are doing well now," he said. "Their journey to *los Estados Unidos de América* cost them their savings and more, but they have applied for citizenship now. Maria is working as a domestic for a good family, and her husband found a job as assistant supervisor for a janitorial firm because he can speak *Inglés.*"

"I don't understand," she said. "Their trip was paid for."

Jorge shrugged. "Señor Riveras told them if they didn't pay the going price, he would have them kicked off the truck."

She went still, again questioning Amando Riveras's motives to help the refugees travel across Mexico unscathed. Had she sought help from a man who was involved in human trafficking?

"I'm glad they are safe now," she said, and earned an enthusiastic nod from Jorge.

If only Miguel had been here to do as he'd promised. But he'd been off in the village helping them. It was time she did what she'd wanted to do all along—be a part of his world.

"Do you know the way to Tumbenkahal?" she asked.

Jorge bobbed his dark head. *"Sí."*

"Then show me how to get there. I need to borrow a vehicle, too," she said.

Jorge fidgeted, seeming instantly wary. "Señor would not like it if you traveled that deeply into the jungle alone."

"Señor wouldn't have liked me helping your family, either, but I did it anyway because he didn't have time to attend to it at the time."

A ruddy flush stained the young man's dark cheeks. "He would dismiss me if he knew."

"Then we won't tell him. Now, Señor Gutierrez needs help." She glanced back to make sure nobody was listening. Still she lowered her voice. "I need to buy water and food and take them to those in need in the village."

His brow creased. "Señor Voltez was to do that."

"Has he left already?"

"*Sí*, but he was going to Tulum first to help his *novia*."

Allegra silently fumed. That trip would take all day, while the Mayans in the jungle waited for supplies.

She smiled at Jorge. "Do you think Señor Gutierrez will be happy his people have been left waiting?"

"No, *señora!*" Jorge said, clearly ill at ease now. "I can't help you access the vehicles stored in the family's garage, but there is an old Jeep behind the gardening shed that I use to buy supplies. It would do well on the muddy roads."

She smiled. "Thank you, Jorge."

"Come," he said, moving away from the house.

"Draw me a map. I must hurry," she said.

Thirty minutes later Allegra drove into Merida to stock up on supplies. She filled the Jeep with provisions, consulted the map Jorge had drawn for her and set off into the jungle.

The Mayans in this region had saved her life six months ago. It was time she paid back their kindness.

CHAPTER EIGHT

THE whine of an engine slashed through the dense jungle like a machete, growing louder as it neared the village. Miguel straightened and swiped the sweat off his brow, his gaze narrowing on the spot where the narrow jungle track opened into the clearing.

Without a doubt a vehicle was churning its way up the trail that was little better than a quagmire following yesterday's torrent that had pounded the Yucatán.

He'd known there would be severe damage. But he hadn't realized the village would be this devastated.

The majority of the huts, farm animals and the crops were now scattered, lost or destroyed. The Mayans had virtually nothing to sustain them for a day, much less a season—not even pure water to drink. But they would soon.

He'd phoned his estate manager and apprised him of the conditions shortly after he'd arrived. Voltez should have dispatched someone here an hour ago with much needed supplies. This had better be him coming up the trail.

But instead of a truck overflowing with supplies, a battered Jeep Cherokee popped over the rise and fishtailed in the mud.

He could barely make out the small driver this far away with the sun glinting on the windshield. Perhaps one of the Mayans who held a job had finally managed to get home.

Miguel returned to the task of helping the men rebuild another hut that had been destroyed, furious the aid he'd promised had not arrived yet.

But a deeper rage burned in him, too, for he couldn't discount Allegra's claim that she'd gotten involved in helping refugees escape Guatemala. How the hell had that happened?

Shouts rose from across the village plaza. "Someone brought in water," said the worker toiling beside him. "Come."

Miguel slid a glance that way and licked his parched lips. He didn't want to deplete the resources brought in to the poor, but he had to hydrate himself, too.

He jabbed his shovel in the mud and started toward the Jeep Cherokee. Halfway there he recognized the vehicle as one of his own. Had Voltez decided to bring the supplies in this?

A bevy of women clustered around the rear of the SUV. He caught the litany of "blessed angel" in Mayan and assumed the women were offering up prayers.

That thought changed when the women moved aside and his gaze fell on the lone Samaritan smiling and handing out bottles of water and small bundles that he assumed were food.

Allegra, here? His wife wore blue jeans that rode low on her hips teamed with a T-shirt that molded to her breasts and nipped in at her narrow waist. She looked incredibly sexy.

And undeniably generous.

He backhanded the sweat from his eyes and stared again, certain his eyes were deceiving him. But no, it was her, his delicate English rose amid a score of natives, standing in mud that ruined her shoes.

"Explain yourself," he said by way of greeting after the crowd thinned and he could get close to her.

"That should be obvious, even to you," she said, not sparing him a glance as she pressed a bottle of water into his hands.

"Who brought you here?"

"Nobody." She straightened and looked at him then, and the fatigue ringing her eyes tore away his spate of anger. "I asked Jorge to draw me a map—"

¡Dios mio! He wanted to wring her neck over risking a drive here though less than hospitable terrain. He wanted to wrap her in his arms and adore her with kisses, for her kindness was something he hadn't expected.

He swore. "I'll dismiss him for this."

"No, you won't," she said, getting in his face. "I asked him for directions, and if he'd have refused, I'd have tried to find my way here anyway."

"Fine, then I will take you home."

"I'm not going anywhere until I've seen that these supplies are disbursed among the people," she said.

He stared at this beautiful, stubborn woman, stunned by her vehemence. "Why are you doing this?"

"They need help." The passionate enthusiasm in her eyes mirrored his own dedication to this cause. "I need to repay the kindness they gave me."

"What are you talking about?"

"The accident. One of the nurses in the Cancún hospital told me that Mayans happened on the accident shortly after it happened." She scanned the people bent to their work and gave a sad smile that made his own breath catch. "If not for them acting so quickly, I'd be dead."

Without another word, she returned to her task of handing out supplies while a new cluster of women emerged from their *palapas*, seeming to know instinctively that help had arrived.

Miguel watched her, still having difficulty believing that she'd been injured—that she'd nearly died. But that would explain her weight loss, as well as the haunted look in her eyes.

If she was telling the truth, then his *madre* had lied to him. He didn't know, but he'd deal with his *madre* later.

Right now he had to decide what to do with the woman who'd just taken it upon herself to do this kindness to his people at great risk to herself. He'd always suspected she possessed this reckless bent. That was why he'd forbidden her to leave the *casa* without a bodyguard.

She'd argued the point then, insisting she didn't need a keeper. That she wouldn't go far.

But he'd learned a painful lesson when he was a boy. Danger lurked everywhere.

He'd failed to protect the brother he'd been charged to watch. He vowed he wouldn't fall short of keeping his wife safe.

But he had. He'd hired a bodyguard who'd not only seduced Allegra, but he'd embroiled her in some scheme to lend aid to refugees fleeing Guatemala. Or was that a lie too?

Miguel wasn't sure who to believe, but he could wring her neck for taking such risks. She should not be volunteering her time when she could dispatch another to do so in her stead.

Very few women he knew, not least his own *madre,* would stand in the sun handing out water and supplies to the *campesinado*. That was far below a noble Castilian.

No, Señora Barrosa was prejudiced against the indigenous people of Mexico, and though he did not believe Allegra would be that narrow-minded, he never dreamed she'd go out of her way to help the Mayans. He'd been so sure of it he'd never given her the chance to prove him wrong.

Yet here she was, smiling at the *campesinado* as she doled out foodstuffs to the women. She was devoid of artifice and full of compassion.

She was his wife, yet he'd never bothered to know this side of her. She was a stranger he found himself attracted to again, only this time it wasn't just carnal interest.

From the beginning he'd let himself believe he was terrified of losing her as he'd lost his brother. But it went deeper than that.

He was terrified of losing control to the overpowering emotions he held for this woman. A love that deep stripped away his defenses and left him vulnerable.

He hated the feeling. He feared it. So he'd denied it. He'd continue denying it, no matter how strong the lure.

"May I help?" he asked as he joined her.

"I'd like that," she said, and rewarded him with a smile that coaxed an answering one from him.

For the better part of an hour, they worked side by side and spoke only to the Mayans who came looking for help. Or rather, to those who came seeking the *ángel de la guarda.*

Working with Allegra let him see a side of her he'd only glimpsed before. She excelled at this, for the people gravitated to her. Miguel caught himself doing the same.

Sí, beyond the desire that simmered in him for her, he admired the strong woman she'd become.

She crouched before a small boy no more than five who'd become separated from his mother. She embraced him and soothed his tears, and something inside Miguel warmed, expanded to chase away the ever-present chill that had filled him for so long.

He wanted her back. Not just in his bed. No, he wanted his wife back in all ways.

That admission was the slap in the face that he needed. Allegra was his passion and his weakness.

He would not blindly fall under her spell and believe her.

"I wish I would have done this before now," she said simply when the little boy spotted his mother and ran to her.

"It would not have been wise in your condition," he said.

"Perhaps so." She shook her head, as if shaking off a memory that plagued her. "How long have you come here to help them?"

He gave a negligent shrug when his body sizzled with annoyance of being thrust in this position of protecting her—of doing as she'd wanted by working and talking. "My *padre* brought me with him when I was young."

Her soft lips parted in a smile. "You never told me about that."

"There was no reason to," he said, because he'd never thought to include her in this part of his life.

Coming here was private. The reasons he worked so hard with the villagers was his alone. He didn't need or want approval, laud or validation.

"How often do you come here?"

"As often as I'm needed," he said. "When there is trouble, I come more often."

"You were here when I left the *casa* that day," she said, a frown pulling at her smooth forehead. "You'd been here for weeks."

"*Sí*, there'd been a horrendous rain and much flooding."

She looked him in the eyes. "I needed you."

He'd needed her, too. Needed her as a husband needed the wife he'd been afraid to touch during the last troubled month of her pregnancy.

The doctor had warned him that she'd had a difficult birth with Cristobel. She needed time to heal before they resumed marital relations.

Yet being around her day and night had driven him mad with desire. He had stopped sharing a bed with her because he was afraid he'd turn to her in the dead of night, that he'd take her without conscious thought to her condition.

That he'd hurt her.

He'd stayed away because he feared that he'd fall more deeply under her spell and lose the edge that had been hammered into him as a boy. So he'd removed the temptation and the danger of causing her harm by coming here to work day and night.

And she'd packed her belongings and left him for another man. Or had she?

She'd returned on the premise that being here would unlock her memory. Closure.

They had to shut the door on that episode of their past before they could open the one to their future. If he could believe her, she'd not taken a lover. She was still his wife.

Still his in all ways!

"When you've finished handing out the supplies, we will return to Hacienda Primaro," he said.

"I thought you had vital work to do here," she said.

"Something far more crucial demands my attention," he said, and before she could ask what, he added, "us."

Allegra had trouble paying attention to her task of dispensing water and supplies after that pronouncement. Just what did he mean? Had he tired of his quest for vengeance and would divorce her now?

Though Miguel was just across the small plaza that was little more than a muddy field, he hadn't looked her way since he dropped that bomb on her. He'd done it again. Shut her out.

It was something that had infuriated her and crushed her during her marriage. She'd wanted to be a part of his life in all ways. She wanted him to talk with her about his plans for their future. She wanted to be more than the mother to his child and the woman in his bed.

But he'd never shared this with her, and it was clear he didn't like doing so now.

Yet she'd felt a different connection flow between them earlier—something besides desire. It was deep and profound and bound them closer than a man and woman. It whispered of a forever kind of love.

But the feeling came and went like the wind. Had she merely imagined it? Was it just wistful thinking?

If it was real, what would it take to bring that closeness they'd shared at the beginning of their affair back to life?

For an hour, Miguel lost himself in hard physical work alongside the other men. Or tried to. More times than not his gaze strayed to Allegra.

Seeing her in this element showed a side of her that he'd never seen before. She was a champion of causes, and it was clear she'd taken up the sword for his people without regard to herself.

Her usual tidy hair was a riot of curls. Her clothes were sweaty and streaked with dirt and mud.

She'd never looked more desirable as a woman.

The temptation to share a hammock with her tonight called to the most primal part of him. But isolating her here with him wouldn't unlock her memories.

They had to confront the past together.

He reached her just as a young couple and an old woman emerged from the jungle, the trio looking haggard and defeated, as if they'd been walking for days. The young man spoke with one of the elders of the village while the women helped the older woman to a bench.

He wasn't surprised when Allegra was the first to take bottled water to the older woman. For a moment, he feared the elder wouldn't take anything from an *Ingles*.

Seeing a white woman here clearly upset the old woman. Her sudden agitation had Allegra moving back, looking startled.

The young man who'd brought the old woman to the village must have noticed, too, for he ran back toward the pair.

Miguel was at Allegra's side in a heartbeat, the instinct to protect her as strong as ever. The old Mayan spoke rapidly, her hands animated, her expression intent as she looked from Allegra to Miguel.

He could scarcely believe his ears. The old woman had to be mistaken. Yet this explained Allegra's flash of memory on the drive to Playa del Carmen.

Allegra had gone pale, despite the flush of sun that stole over her skin. "What is she saying?"

He was loath to tell her, but lying served no purpose, either. Both of them had been kept in the dark far too long regarding the accident.

Accident? Not if the elder could be believed.

"She claims she saw the accident," Miguel said.

"No! *En que el conductor se da a la fuga.*" The young man standing beside the elder frowned.

Allegra gripped Miguel's arm, her fingernails digging into his flesh. "What do you mean?"

The young man glanced nervously to Miguel as if asking his permission to explain. Miguel nodded for him to go on, for though Allegra understood *Español*, she'd never grasped all of the regional nuances.

"A hit and run, *señora*," the young man said. "The car rammed into yours and you lost control."

Allegra pinched her eyes shut and inhaled so sharply his lungs tightened in empathy. "You are positive he hit me?"

"*Sí, señora,*" the young man said. "It happened right as you reached the *topes*."

"I can't remember it," she said.

For once, Miguel wondered if that wasn't a blessing.

Allegra was a competent driver, but it would have taken lightning quick reflexes to control a car in such a situation. She'd failed and paid a horrific price for leaving him, all because a man had been driving recklessly and caused her to wreck the car.

She turned to him, and her confusion tore at his heart. "Uncle Loring didn't say anything about a car hitting mine."

"How could he have known?" he asked, loath to offer any defense of the man who'd lied to him about Allegra's injuries.

She faced the young man, the frustration in her eyes mirroring his own. "What happened after the collision?"

"The driver stopped," the young man said. "He went to the car and opened the back door."

Where Miguel's *niña* was strapped in her car seat, sleeping the sleep of death. "You are sure he opened the rear door first?"

"*Sí*. He glanced at the driver, then he kicked the door shut, returned to his car and sped off." The young man frowned. "Grandmother thought he went for help."

"But he didn't," Miguel said as a darker possibility for this tragedy slammed into him.

The young man shook his head. "No, *señor*. I ran to the next village and called *la polica*. They told me I was the only one who'd alerted them of the accident."

¡Dios mio! Had the man panicked when he'd realized a woman and baby had died? Or was it as Miguel feared—the man made a clumsy attempt to kidnap either Cristobel or Allegra, and after the accident, realized Miguel's *niña* was dead and his wife was clinging to life?

"Can you describe the driver," Allegra asked, a frantic edge to her voice now.

"He was a Mexican," the young man said. "Very thin. Close cut black hair." He shrugged, as if indicating that's all he could provide.

That description matched half the male population in Mexico. "Do you remember his car?"

The young man nodded. "*Sí*. It was white, a Jetta."

"I've seen that car," Allegra said, pinching her eyes shut as if trying to dredge up the memory, only to shake her head in a sign of frustration he now recognized.

"Where?" he asked.

She shook her head, then went still. Her gaze lifted to his, wary and questioning. "At Hacienda Primaro."

"You are sure?"

"Yes, but I can't imagine an employee of yours doing something so deadly horrific."

He could. He'd learned at a young age that those in his family's employ weren't immune to the lure of a small fortune gained from a kidnapping. But to realize that his family had lost two children to kidnappers...

A stinging sense of ineptitude needled him. He'd known the possibility of such a tragedy befalling his family again was there even with all the precautions he'd made at the hacienda. That's why he'd hired Riveras. That's why he was so vehement that Allegra never leave the *casa* alone.

But he hadn't factored in an unfaithful wife, or a deceitful employee. Who'd made the first overture—Riveras or Allegra?

And why the hell hadn't Riveras gone with Allegra that day? Why had he allowed her to leave the hacienda alone?

"Gracias," he said to the young man, then led Allegra toward his Jeep with renewed determination to get to the truth.

"What are you going to do?" Allegra asked.

"Find out if your defiance played into a kidnapper's plans," he said.

"A kidnapper?" She flinched and pressed trembling fingers to her temples, a whisper of distress escaping her. "My God! You think that's why I was run off the road?"

"Sí, and you made it easy for him by leaving the *casa* alone." He curled his fingers into fists to keep from reaching for her. "Why didn't Riveras accompany you, *querida*?"

"I don't know," she said, her voice small and her gaze troubled. "I remember Cristobel cried out. I glanced in the rearview mirror and recall a sense of terror." She shook her head and swallowed hard. "I don't remember anything else, but that must be when the car slammed into me."

"*Sí,* you crashed and likely lost consciousness," he said. And Cristobel's death ended the kidnapper's ploy.

Instead of calling for help, the bastard ran. He left Allegra there to die.

Miguel couldn't stand it any longer and pulling her close enfolded her in his arms, absorbing her tremors as well as his own. His heart beat too fast and too loud, like a native drum heralding war.

This was war. He couldn't bring back his daughter or regain what he'd lost with Allegra, but he would hunt down the coward who destroyed his family.

He would make him pay.

As for Allegra?

He'd do all in his power to find the key that would unlock her memory. For she'd left him. She'd placed herself and their *niña* in danger.

It was fitting revenge that her failure would vividly haunt her the rest of her days.

Allegra was so weary from the day's work that she fell asleep in the car. For someone who'd napped in fits and starts the past six months, dozing off now was unbelievable.

As usual, it wasn't a long or restful sleep.

The same thing woke her as always—Cristobel crying as she raced down the Merida Libre. She'd wanted to take the *autopista,* but she'd gotten in the wrong lane.

An overwhelming sense of fear clawed at her, as if she was running for her life. Cristobel was fussy, weary from the trip already.

She'd glanced in the rearview mirror and her heart clenched at that precious little face scrunched red with displeasure. Her first instinct was to pull over and see to her baby and then retrace her route to the *autopista* that would get her to Cancún much quicker. But the sudden revving of an engine behind her brought her gaze flicking up to the rearview mirror.

The white car was riding her bumper. Her gaze lifted to the driver just as the car slammed into them.

Her head snapped forward, her hands grappling to control the car. Terror engulfed her as the car flipped. Once. Twice.

Metal crunched. Glass shattered. Cristobel screamed.

Pain skewered Allegra, then silence settled over her a heartbeat before she fell into a blessed blackness where there was no pain.

"Why are you scowling?" Miguel asked.

"I remembered the accident again," she said. "But I don't know why I was driving to Cancún."

Miguel muttered a curse and whipped his gaze back to the road, his proud profile tensed in fury. "That is obvious. You were leaving me."

"No, I wasn't," she said, her own anger spiking when he persisted in believing that lie.

"You are certain of this because?"

"Because I loved you," she said, never doubting that certainty.

Her words echoed in the charged silence that pulsed in the thick, sultry air. Miguel stared straight ahead, his powerful body tense and his chiseled features so resolute that she wanted to scream in frustration.

She couldn't deal with being here with Miguel, wanting him as much as ever, knowing he cared nothing for her but anger.

"I wouldn't have left you," she said again, willing him to believe the truth—to believe her.

His expression turned fierce, though the heat in his eyes hinted of a passionate rage that her body recognized and responded to in a heartbeat. "But you did. You packed your belongings, took our daughter and left the *casa*."

"For a day or two at the most," she said. "I was going to the beach house. I'm certain of it now."

A fire lit his obsidian eyes in a lightning flash of anger that sparked her own irritation. "Then why did you take a fortune in jewels with you?"

"I didn't!"

The air between them crackled with raw energy that left her trembling with frustration. Why couldn't he believe her just once? Why did he persist in thinking the worst of her?

He stared at her for a long time, his features hard and remote, revealing nothing of his emotions, his thoughts. With a muttered curse, he focused his attention on driving.

She hated that he distanced himself from her again. He'd always had that ability to school his emotions, a necessary tool in his business dealings, but a slap in the face to the wife who simply wanted to share her thoughts with her husband.

"Fine! Shut me out of your life again. I don't care who you believe," she said, which was a lie.

She cared too much, for if he couldn't trust, then all they had between them was this sizzling sexual attraction. Perhaps that's all they'd ever had.

Could she have misjudged this man so?

A deep growl rumbled from him. "Okay, why did you leave? Tell me so I understand why you placed yourself and our *niña* in great danger."

She blew out an exasperated breath and voiced what she felt certain of. "I was running away from Riveras, not you."

He cut her a look that conveyed his doubts of that claim. "You were seen arguing with him the morning you left."

"Yes, I was angry that he'd charged Jorge's family more

money for their journey north." She frowned, annoyed that she couldn't remember that last incident. "He wasn't a good man."

He strangled the steering wheel so hard the tendons roped on his bare, bronzed arms. "Damn Riveras for failing to protect you! For involving you in what sounds like human trafficking."

Silence roared between them, for what could she say when he put it like that? She should've realized Riveras wasn't helping the refugees out of the goodness of his heart.

She'd returned for answers, but was more confused than before. Someone had tried to kidnap Cristobel. Perhaps her as well. Her going off without Amando played into their hands.

"I don't blame you for hating me," she said.

"Do not put words in my mouth, *querida*."

"Because I hate myself," she went on, ignoring his order. "If I hadn't left the *casa* with Cristobel alone, she'd still be alive. We'd have a chance of making our marriage work."

He swore an oath that made her blush. "Then hate me as well, for if I'd have hired a competent guard, he'd have stopped you from leaving. He wouldn't have seduced you."

She shook her head, sad that he believed she'd been unfaithful. There was nothing left for her here now.

Miguel was right when he'd said their marriage ended with Cristobel's death. She wasn't even sure she'd find the closure she'd sought, for much of her memory was still trapped in a fog.

"There is no going back to what we had," she said.

"No."

"So do we simply enjoy our farewell fling for a few more days?" she asked, her heart heavy at the thought of finally ending what had begun with such promise. Never mind that she'd come back for that very reason—closure.

"No. We start over."

CHAPTER NINE

"ARE you out of your mind?" she asked, her voice oddly strained.

"I want you." He slid her a sultry glance that brought color to her pale cheeks. "And you want me."

She gaped, then bit her lower lip and stared out the side window. "I never said that."

"Not in so many words."

"Not in any words."

He ground his teeth together, knowing he'd taken the wrong tactic with her. His English rose was growing prickly again. But then she'd always become defensive when she was afraid.

"Answer me this," he said, not about to let this drop now that he'd made the decision. "Were you leaving me that day?"

"No," she said, sounding exasperated again.

"Then it is settled," he said.

The decision felt right. He didn't know how long this intense desire for her would last, but she was still his wife, and he wasn't ready to walk away from her.

She let out a troubled groan. "It is not settled! We have too much unsaid between us to jump back into marriage."

"Then we will do as I was remiss in doing throughout our marriage and talk at length," he said, putting an end to that argument with glacial arrogance.

She stared at him as if she was seeing him for the very first time. "You're serious."

"Totally. Our families lied to us. If they hadn't interfered, we wouldn't have been separated the past six months." He held her wary gaze with his. "If they'd minded their business, we would have grieved our *niña*'s passing together instead of apart."

She tore her gaze from his, clearly apprehensive about giving their marriage another chance.

"For someone who complained we didn't talk, you are being awfully quiet." She looked on the verge of tears, too, but he wasn't about to mention it.

"I'm thinking." And worrying her hands to death which wasn't a good sign at all. "Staying married is a big step."

"It was the same step we took the first time," he said, daring her to argue.

"I was pregnant then. You married me out of duty."

He sieved air through his clenched teeth. "We are still married! I will not grant you a divorce until I am ready to bury what burns so hotly between us."

She cupped her hands over her face, aware that arguing with him was a waste of breath. But she couldn't just capitulate, either, not on something this important. Not when her heart was in danger of being broken all over again.

"I can never give you children," she said, voicing an admission of her own.

"I am not asking that of you."

She nodded, understanding what he did expect from her. Sex. They'd enjoy each other for however long it lasted, and she'd have a broken heart to heal all over again.

She peered at him over the tips of her fingers. "Do you finally believe I was faithful to you?"

His answer cracked like lightning. "It means I intend to

make love to you so thoroughly and so deeply that you'll forget what it was like to lie in another man's arms."

He maneuvered the Jeep along the jungle track, acutely aware of each breath, each tense movement Allegra made. They used to share a congenial silence, but this one crackled with tension that played over his nerves in sharp, angry discords.

"I won't live with a man who distrusts me," she said at last.

"*Sí*, you will," he said. "Do not attempt to play the injured party here for I have proof that you and Amando left the *casa* every day, taking a picnic basket with you on your assignation."

"Proof? You have nothing. That picnic basket was filled with food for the refugees," she said, her voice rising this time with biting disgust.

Ah, yes, her charity work for the Mayans. The thought of her aiding the natives strummed cords of fear in him, but on its heels boiled rage at the guard he'd hired for letting his wife take such a risk.

This time he was going to get some answers. He'd not be deterred this time.

"How the hell did you get involved in that?" he asked.

"Through Jorge."

"The boy who foolishly drew you the map to Tumbenkahal?"

"One and the same, and I'll hold you to your promise to let him be."

He dipped his chin in agreement, secretly admiring that she'd secured his promise before he learned all the details. "Go on."

"When I was in the garden reading one day, Jorge told me about relatives of his who were trying to escape Guatemala," she said. "I asked what could be done, and he said you'd promised to look into it some months past."

"That should have been the end of your involvement into *my* business," he said, getting angry all over again.

"Well, they'd managed to make it this far on into Mexico

on their own, and I couldn't turn my back on them," she said, the passion in her voice leaving no doubt she was serious.

"You should have come to me with your concerns," he said.

She glared at him. "You weren't there."

He ground his teeth, for he had no argument to challenge that very real fact. He'd left Amando Riveras to keep her safe. He didn't doubt she'd rushed to help others in need, just as she had by delivering water and supplies to Tumbenkahal.

"Exactly how did you go about helping the refugees?" he asked.

She smiled, but it was tinged with worry. "In the beginning I set about teaching Jorge's sister and brother-in-law English. It was a trial because they only spoke Mayan, but once we got past the basics, they learned quickly."

"When and where did you conduct this school?" he asked, holding a tight rein on the pride swelling within him for his wife's generosity.

She shifted uneasily, and he knew before she opened her mouth that he wasn't going to like what she said. "I followed the an old henequen trail to the far edge of the jungle."

"You had better say that Riveras accompanied you."

Her eyes wouldn't meet his. "He did on occasion."

Sweat beaded on his brow. Sweat caused from fear of the danger she placed herself in!

"I told Amando about their plight, and he said he often helped those less fortunate escape Guatemala," she went on. "In fact, within two weeks there were close to twenty-five more refugees hiding near the hut."

Rage exploded in him, but a good deal was directed at himself. For he knew what Riveras was doing. He knew he'd misjudged the man badly. He'd placed his family and his own workers in danger by bringing Riveras here.

To think that Allegra had gone off into the jungle with him…

"*¡Maldita sea!* Riveras was using Hacienda Primaro as the holding ground for his human trafficking scheme." If the authorities had discovered a refugee camp on his land, the blot on his family name would have been devastating and caused him no end of trouble in his business dealings.

"I realized what he was doing belatedly, too. I needed to tell you what he was doing, but you'd gone off and nobody knew where," she said, rubbing her brow that was now puckered with worry as she remembered more and more. "He frightened me, Miguel. He frightened me so that I packed up Cristobel and left."

Guilt danced hand in hand with his anger. He'd phoned home two days before the accident to talk with Allegra. He'd intended to tell her to be ready to go on an extended trip, but she wasn't home.

According to his *madre* she'd gone off with Riveras again on their daily picnic that usually lasted most of the day. She'd let him draw his own conclusion.

Hindsight was always right. He should have gone home then and confronted Riveras. He should have had faith in his marriage and his wife.

But she'd ditched one lover for him when she'd first come to the Yucatán. And considering his own failed affair with the unfaithful Tara, he had no wish to confront his errant wife when his rage and hurt were towering.

So he'd gone off to nurse his wounds and plan his next attack. A mistake he'd regret until his dying day.

"Where are you taking me?" she asked, staring out the window at the thickening jungle.

He smiled though the gesture held no comfort. "Home."

Sunlight flickered through the breaks in the dense canopy like an old movie reel, teasing him with memories of him working endlessly on the old hacienda he'd lovingly restored. It stood on the fringe of the jungle, stood as a memorial to a marriage gone wrong.

He'd restored it for Allegra. The grand surprise to gift his English rose on their anniversary.

It stood unfinished, a testament now to what lay uncompleted between them. This was a fitting place to end this uncertainty eating at them both.

It was vitally important to him that she know he hadn't put business above her and Cristobel. That he hadn't intentionally let her down as she'd accused him of doing. That he'd physically worked on this house like his ancestors had done for the women that had stolen their hearts.

"Did I ever tell you that I'm equally drawn to and terrified of the jungle?" she asked, a frown pulling at her brow.

He smiled, remembering. "*Sí*. The first time I brought you to Hacienda Primaro you clung to me like one of the spider monkeys frolicking in the banyan trees."

She blushed. "You must have thought me silly."

"No, for I know well the allure and danger of the jungle."

A comfortable silence drifted on the humid air thick with the smell of damp earth and spicy-sweet exotic flowers. Early in their relationship he'd taken her on long drives across the peninsula to show her the world of his ancestors.

She made few remarks, seeming to prefer absorbing the exquisite wonder of nature around them, preferring to snuggle close to him and just share the same oneness nature gifted on them.

The long drives solidified the fact that they could speak without words. A look. A smile. A touch—he knew what she wanted and when she wanted it.

Yet he'd misjudged her in the worst way after Cristobel was born. He was an astute businessman. His instincts for guessing a rival's moves had enabled him to amass a fortune.

So why hadn't he realized his wife was lonely?

"Your blood is strong, Miguel."

He glanced at her, perplexed. "Meaning?"

"I always equated you to your ancestors who came here to conquer." She frowned down at the hands clasped tightly in her lap. "You are a modern conquistador."

"Is that a compliment or an insult?" he asked.

She loosed a soft laugh that rolled in like the tide, then ebbed to draw him to her—toward danger. "A bit of both, perhaps. You couldn't have amassed what you did if you hadn't had the temerity and wits to achieve your goals."

He failed to see the negative in that observation, but he wasn't about to argue the point and spoil this rare mood. He'd been born into this life, but he'd wanted more than to manage it. He'd wanted to make his own mark on the world.

"Today I saw another side of you." She tipped her head to look at him, either unaware just how charming she appeared or deliberately tempting him. "You would fit the role of a tribal leader. Or perhaps a Mayan warrior."

"You think this because?" he asked, bemused that she'd recognized those familiar links.

"Your arrogance for one."

"I am not arrogant."

"You are," she said, seeming not the least reserved to bring that to his attention. "You think that we can save our marriage."

"And you do not?"

She shook her head, her eyes dimming with sadness. "Oddly enough it was your unparalleled confidence in yourself that attracted me to you."

"Here I thought it was my devastating good looks that turned your head."

"That, too," she said, a slow smile teasing her lips that he longed to claim.

Soon, he thought.

Miguel leaned back in the seat, relaxing at last. He had missed this banter with her nearly as much as he'd missed her kisses, her caresses, her fathomless passion when they made love.

He noticed the faded yellow stripes on the *topes* nearly too late. "Brace yourself," he said as he slammed on the brakes, skidding on the blacktop like a *turista* unaware of the speed bumps.

Allegra yelped and slammed both hands on the dashboard, staring at the windshield as if a chilling movie were playing out before her. Her chest rose and fell rapidly, her skin blanched too pale, her blue eyes were far too wide.

He pulled to the dirt lot of the village *abarrotería* and stopped, attuned to the signs of her distress. "What do you see?"

She frowned and shook her head, likely annoyed his voice had intruded on her memory. "The same as before. Cristobel crying right before the white Jetta rammed my car. But this time I saw the driver's face. It was Amando Riveras."

"You are certain?"

"Yes, it was him," she said. "He followed me because he knew I intended to find you. My God! He wanted to kill me, Miguel."

Anguish like he'd never known engulfed him as he put the Jeep in gear and continued on. All this time he'd blamed Allegra for placing her life and Cristobel's in danger by fleeing Hacienda Primaro on a lark. For slipping past the guard he'd hired to protect her.

Never once had he thought the man he'd hired had intentionally caused the accident. Had Riveras feared his retribution once Allegra told him what he was illegally doing? Was he insanely jealous of Allegra and vowed if he couldn't have her, nobody could?

Whatever the reason, he'd better hope Miguel never found him. For he'd never let this wrong go unpunished. *Never!*

He took a sharp left turn onto a paved driveway choked with greenery so dense that the fronds brushed the sides of the Jeep as he passed through. If one wasn't looking closely, they'd miss the driveway entirely, which had been his intention of designing it thusly.

Protection from onlookers, yet the idea of being so careful mocked him now.

The driveway curved around a thicket of mangrove, the vegetation cut back farther and farther from the road until they emerged into a clearing artfully landscaped with tropical plants. The *casa principia* was smaller than many other main homes on the old haciendas, but the intimate size suited his taste better than the rambling *casa* he'd grown up in.

He pulled around back and parked, mindful of Allegra's gasp of surprise. This view always took his breath away as well, for the portico ran the length of the house, and with the setting sun bathing the stucco a warm gold, it looked like a Mayan palace fit for a king.

"It's beautiful," she said.

He took no pleasure in her compliment, for he'd designed this with Allegra in mind. Everything here reminded him of her—a constant torment he hadn't cared to live with—the reason why he'd not been able to finish this as he'd dreamed of doing.

And now? Now he was starting anew with the wife he'd wronged. The woman who expected more of him this time. A woman who deserved far more than he was willing to give her.

"Gracias." Miguel bounded from the Jeep to assist her and entwined his fingers with hers to anchor her close, to feel her accelerated pulse streak into him.

"What is this place?" she asked.

"An old hacienda that I've restored," he said, because he couldn't bring himself to admit to her that this was to be their *casa*. Not yet, anyway.

"How long have you owned it?" she asked, clearly enthralled.

"A little over two years."

She looked away, but he caught the hurt in her eyes that he'd kept this from her. "This is one of the haciendas you've restored then as a luxury rental retreat."

"No," he said, watching her face closely. "This was to be a surprise for you."

He knew the second when understanding dawned, for her eyes widened and her inviting mouth parted. She scanned the length of the house before turning to him.

"You bought this for us?"

"Sí." He lifted his gaze to the restored portico and plaster-work, painfully aware this restoration was nothing compared to the extensive work done inside the *casa.* "This is where I spent my free time the last months of your pregnancy. I wanted the *casa* ready before Cristobel was born, but a tropical storm set back my plans."

"You were gone so much," she said, and he nodded in reply for there was nothing he could say or do in the face of all he'd done wrong. "You should have told me."

"Would that have made you happy?"

"No." She lifted a hand and cupped his jaw, and the jolt of her touch rocked him to his soul. "Knowing you'd done this for us is wonderful. But just being with you made me happy, Miguel. I only wanted to be more than the woman in your bed. I wanted to be the one you confided in. Why can't you see that?"

What he saw was a woman who wanted to know the minutiae of his business just to satisfy her curiosity. It made no sense to him and until it did, he'd remain cautious.

"It is difficult to alter the way I've lived for so long."

And her smile turned down at that, but she didn't comment.

He took his purchases from the Jeep and nodded to the house. "Come. The hour grows late and I am weary."

"How long will we stay here?" she asked, matching him step for step as they strode down the long portico.

"As long as it pleases us."

Allegra faltered, her knees going weak for she knew he was going to go all out to seduce her. And God knew she was ravenous for his kiss, his touch, his possession.

She'd take what he offered, knowing it could all end too swiftly. She'd love him like there was no tomorrow. And when it ended this time, she'd return to England with her memories and regrets.

This would be an all-out seduction meant to erode her last defenses. Surely pride goaded Miguel to make his mark on her again, to obliterate any other lover from her mind, which was simple to do since she'd had only one other man in her life and that memory was so vague it was laughable.

Her own pride begged her to resist, but she was powerless to resist Miguel for he was offering her what she'd longed for most. Her husband. Their own house. The promise of tomorrow.

Everything but a child, and that she couldn't give him.

But for however long they were here she could pretend that their differences had been laid to rest. That he trusted her. Loved her.

He twined his fingers with hers and led her through an ornately arched doorway into the main hall. She was sure she'd never seen a more splendid arrangement of earthen colors and plush appointments in her life. It was exactly what she would have picked out, which proved he'd known her well.

At least in this regard.

"Make yourself comfortable," he said as he put the perishables away. "The housekeeper didn't know to expect us, so you'll have to content yourself until I walk to her *casita* and bring her back here."

"Don't bother on my account. I can prepare a light meal."

For a long moment she thought he'd argue, but he gave a curt nod and released her. "Very well. I'm going to the cenote at the edge of the lawn for a swim. Join me?"

"I didn't bring a bathing suit," she said.

He quirked one dark eyebrow. "Good. I would prefer you naked in my arms."

The challenge was there. And what would she do here alone while he took a swim? Shower and wash her soiled clothes. Putter about the kitchen waiting for him to return. Dwell on him out there in the water, gloriously naked and alone.

The electronic trill from his mobile echoed in the cavernous room. Before he dug it from his pocket, the amorous glint in his eyes was replaced by a mien of cool reserve.

"What have you discovered?" he asked the caller, all the while holding her in place with the intensity in his gaze.

She went still, guessing this had to do with her.

"You are certain of this?" Miguel said, a slice of surprise cutting through his dark expression. "No, that is all for now."

He laid his phone on the desk in a deceptively relaxed movement that didn't fool her one bit. For one glance at the muscle pounding in his cheek confirmed he was beyond angry.

"Well?" she asked when her nerves threatened to snap in the tense lapse of silence.

"Your uncle had you admitted into Bartholomew Fields."

"I told you that," she said.

"He had no right." He thumped a fist on his chest. "I am your husband. If you needed medical care, I should have been consulted."

She had no argument for that. How different things would have been if Loring had contacted Miguel. And why in the world hadn't he?

Surely he'd heard her cry for Miguel often during that

time. Just what had her uncle said to the doctors when he'd had her admitted into Bartholomew Fields?

"He will pay for his interference," Miguel said.

"No, he won't," she said, bracing herself for an argument. "He likely was only doing what he felt was best for me."

He smacked his palms on the smooth tiled counter. "Do not defend your uncle to me!"

She fisted her hands, so angry at this proud, jealous man she could scream. "Why not? He took over my care because you weren't around. He talked to me on the phone, Miguel. He knew I was miserable at Hacienda Primaro. He was well aware you'd left me there to birth your heir while you went on with your life!"

"The hacienda was our home until I could complete this one," he said.

She pressed a hand over her heart. "I didn't know that. I knew nothing of your plans or where you were at, but I knew someone did because you arrived at the hospital for Cristobel's birth. Then too soon you were gone again."

He waved a hand as if dismissing her outrage. "We have been over this before."

"Who did know, Miguel?" she asked. "Your mother?"

A muscle worked frantically along his jaw. "She knew if I wasn't here, I was working on the project in Tumbenkahal."

"Yet you didn't confide in your wife."

"It was to be a surprise," he said, impatience vibrating in his deep voice. "Besides, what difference does it make now?"

"Trust," she said simply. "A husband should trust his wife and you obviously never did."

A dark scowl pulled at his arrogant features for it was obvious Miguel had trust issues with her. "You gave me no reason to believe you, and many to raise doubts."

It was time to let this topic go, but she couldn't. There were too many unanswered questions. Too much hurt.

"Why didn't your mother contact you right after the accident? Why didn't she send a servant out to tell you that your wife was clinging to life and your baby was dead?"

His complexion turned ashen. "I was out of the country and couldn't be contacted."

His face and shoulders were so tensed up she could see the anger eddying off him in waves. "I don't doubt you were severely injured, *querida*. Know that I won't be forgiving to the man who locked my wife away from me for six months."

She pressed both palms over the hard, unyielding wall of his chest. "I won't let you harm Uncle Loring."

He flashed her a ferocious scowl. "Why not?"

"He is retired and living off a modest pension," she said softly. "I know he spent a considerable amount of his money ensuring I received the best care."

"So I'm to forgive your uncle for his deception because he's old and he used his money to care for you when your husband could have bought the whole hospital?"

"Yes! Your revenge is meaningless, because if you'd truly wanted to find me, Miguel," she said, voicing the truth that had filled her with desolation for so long, "then you would have found me. You wouldn't have given up unless you'd wanted to."

With that, she left the room with as much dignity as she could. But her heart ached with the awful truth she'd just voiced. And it was the truth.

He had investigators at his disposal that could have found her. Even if her uncle had placed her in Bartholomew Fields, someone who worked there would have talked for the right monetary incentive.

He simply hadn't wanted to find her.

The rapid thud of his shoes on the tiles alerted her that

Miguel was fast on her heels. She steeled herself for more arguing and picked up her pace, for in truth she was weary of hashing over the same thing that left them circling the issue—he didn't trust her.

"All right," he said. "I will leave your uncle in peace if you stay with me."

She whipped around to face him, furious he was blackmailing her to remain with him. "You can't be serious."

"I mean every word," he said. "You stay with me and Loring Vandohrn will continue to enjoy his retirement. Leave and I'll ruin him."

"Fine, I'll stay with you, but until you learn to trust me, I'm nothing more than your whore."

With that, she went in search of the kitchen, thankful her steps sounded sure and steady when she was feeling anything but positive.

She half expected Miguel to follow and pick up the thread of the argument again. But she heard the door open and close and knew he'd stepped outside.

Good! Hopefully a swim in the cenote would soothe his ill temper, and the separation would give her time to cool her annoyance with him.

But he hadn't returned in the thirty minutes it took her to prepare a light dinner. When fifteen more minutes passed with only the chatter of spider monkeys and caw of exotic birds echoing from the jungle, worry dug claws into her.

She looked out the window, concerned over what was taking him so long. Was he lost in the moment of swimming? Or had some ill befallen him?

The latter seemed far-fetched, but the probability wouldn't leave her. She chewed her lower lip, debating what to do. Waiting for him to return held no appeal for her.

He'd asked her to join him earlier. Dare she?

She didn't know, could barely think over the worry pounding away in her head. One thing was clear: She couldn't stand here waiting any longer.

CHAPTER TEN

ALLEGRA pushed out the door and hurried along the portico, the click of her sandals hushing the cacophony in the jungle. She paused at the end of the portico and splayed her hands on the stucco column. "Miguel?"

An eerie silence pulsed in the thick, humid air.

She stared at the shadows crouched across the lawn and gave in to a shiver. The cenote must be back there, not far from the house. Surely it wouldn't take long to walk to it.

She scanned the well-tended garden for a sign of life, but nobody was around but her. Bucking up her courage, she struck out across the stone path and welcomed the excitement of her finding Miguel in a pool, gloriously naked.

In moments she stood at the top of the chasm, staring down at the placid surface of water that looked more black than turquoise this time of day. The last rays of light skipped down the flight of wooden steps that led to the shelf far below.

"Miguel? Are you down there?"

She scanned the shelf and clusters of rock, growing more worried when he failed to answer her. She started down the flight, her fingers tightening around the wooden rail that had been sanded smooth from use.

She sensed more than saw that she was alone. The quiet vibrated around her as if alive, raising the hair at her nape.

Twilight fell instantly, as if a giant hand had turned off the sun. She hurried back up the stairs and stumbled into the clearing cloaked in shadows.

The *casa*, which had seemed relatively close before, loomed an eternity away now. Long, thin shadows stretched out from the dense foliage like gnarled fingers.

The jungle changed at night, coming alive with a different energy. Mysterious. Alluring. Dangerous.

She set off across the lawn, her gaze focused on the glow of light drifting from beneath the portico.

The whisper of boughs parting in the dense greenery behind her feathered chills up her limbs. Something was back there, watching her. Dare she run?

"Allegra!" Miguel's tone cracked with authority and a tinge of concern that further shattered her calm.

She turned back to the house and spotted him beneath the portico. His tall, imposing shadow offered no calm.

"Coming," she shouted, picking up her pace.

"Do not run!" The order brooked no argument.

In moments, an engine echoed from the *casa*. The Jeep's headlights moved toward her in a zigzag course, as if the driver were in his cups as he bathed the lawn in swaths of light.

She continued walking toward him, back straight, heart pounding with relief. All was well now. They'd simply crossed paths somehow.

The Jeep skidded to a stop just beyond her.

"Get in," Miguel ordered, his voice as hard as bedrock.

She didn't argue. "Thank you. Darkness came over me before I realized it."

"You shouldn't be out here alone."

"I thought you were swimming in the cenote."

He threw the Jeep in gear and they jolted off. "I was, but I knew the danger in staying there past dark."

"I was on my way back to the house," she said. "No harm done."

He huffed out a breath tinged with disgust. "This area is far more primitive than Hacienda Primaro. The land borders the reserve. That jungle is home to jaguar and puma, and the big cats are always looking for an easy meal."

She digested that news slowly, letting a deeper meaning sink in. When it did, her anger exploded again.

"You intended to bring our daughter to this deserted place where jaguar roam free?"

"She would have been guarded at all times, just as she was at Hacienda Primaro."

A chill slid down her spine. "Have you forgotten that your former guard was the one who rammed my car?"

"No." He stared straight ahead, the lights of the dashboard illuminating the chiseled line of his stubborn jaw. "I will not forget that he murdered our daughter. And so you know," he said with emphasis, "I have hired detectives to find Amando Riveras and bring him back here."

"You'll let the police and courts handle it." She held her breath, hoping he'd say yes.

"*Sí*, he will be handed over to the proper authorities." His dark gaze dared her to disagree.

"He deserves what he gets." For if Riveras hadn't rear-ended her and sent her car out of control, she'd still have her daughter. She'd still be able to have more babies. Blinking back tears she looked away.

Miguel parked the car near the portico and cut the engine. He gave the *casa* a glance filled with such longing that she knew he'd fallen in love with this place. What surprised her was that it appealed to her as well. If only their other difficulties could be put to rest.

"Come," he said, opening her door and extending his hand to her.

She hesitated a heartbeat before laying her palm in his. Heat spread up her arm, the sense of oneness making her tremble.

"I prepared a cold plate of meats and cheeses for dinner," she said as he escorted her into the house.

He didn't release her hand. "I am not hungry for food."

An intense energy hummed between them, keeping her senses honed sharp, her desire soaring. Even if he'd give her the option to postpone lovemaking, she wanted him too much to refuse.

Yes, they were hiding from the real issues still. But perhaps that was for the best, for in bed their bodies spoke freely.

His thumb lightly stroked her hand in that way that always precluded him drawing her to him. Claiming her mouth, her body.

He the conqueror, and she always surrendered to him.

She loved this man. She'd always loved him, even though he'd hurt her unbearably, even though there was only one need she could serve for him now.

Admitting that broke her heart all over again. Still she wanted him more than her next breath.

He slid both arms around her and pulled her flush with him, his eyes gleaming with desire and some other emotion she couldn't read.

He dropped a kiss on her forehead that left her trembling.

She'd be his willing wife for eternity, if only he'd believe her. But as long as he withheld his trust from her, as long as he shut her out of his life, their marriage would never work.

They were right back where they started as lovers. She doubted he'd have married her if she hadn't gotten pregnant.

She twisted from his arms and walked to the fireplace that lay as suddenly cold as her hopes and dreams.

"Have you changed your mind?" he asked, coming up to her from behind, not touching her physically but his heat reached out to her all the same.

"No," she answered at last, turning to face him. "I just want to be sure I am prepared for the risk we're taking."

"¡Estupendo!" He took a box from the paper bag he'd set on the credenza and tossed it on the sofa. "This should be more than enough to still your fears."

She stared at the box of condoms and wanted to laugh. Is that what he thought worried her?

Though her monthly cycle was like clockwork, it was simply a painful taunt. She couldn't begin to remember how many nights she'd cried herself to sleep, despondent that she'd never conceive again, devastated that she'd lost her darling daughter.

"I told you before that I was badly injured in the accident," she said. "I can't conceive."

Miguel jammed his fists into his pockets and watched her face for evidence of deceit, but read nothing but profound sorrow line her features and dim the glow in her eyes. The angst in her voice clawed at his heart.

"This was confirmed by a doctor?" he asked.

Her laugh was bitter. "Yes, in Cancún after the surgery. They had to remove an ovary that had ruptured, and then infection set in." She hugged herself and shivered, and he knew at that moment she spoke the truth. "Another specialist in England confirmed that I'd never conceive without more surgery, and even then the chances were remote."

A quiet rage built in Miguel, for his *madre* should have told him this as soon as he'd absorbed the tragedy of his *niña's* death. But he'd been fed a litany of accusations about Allegra's infidelity. He'd been led to believe she'd taken the small fortune in jewels to fund her affair with Riveras.

The lies were woven with the facts to form an intricate mantilla. One couldn't see the flaw unless they examined the whole carefully. And to his shame he hadn't exhausted all resources during the past six months.

He'd fed on revenge to assuage his grief. No more.

"Then we won't need condoms," he said.

"You believe me?" she asked, a wealth of hope riding on that question.

"*Sí.*

"I will have my secretary find the best infertility clinic and have him make an appointment for us as soon as possible," he said, and knew that was the wrong thing to say the moment the words left his mouth for it sounded as if he was more interested in having another child rather than repairing the massive tear in his marriage.

She stiffened and took a step back. "Even if it was possible, the last thing I want to do with you is have another child right now."

¡Dios mio! Why must she blow this out of proportion? "You love children. Don't deny you want to have another."

"I'm not, but there is too much unsettled between us to even think of being parents again."

"Then let's settle it now."

She tossed both arms upward as if that was the stupidest suggestion he could make. And maybe it was for how could they come to terms with six months of lies and half-truths?

"Why do you want me to remain your wife?" she asked.

It was a trick question and one he wasn't about to answer blithely. "We are good together."

She laughed. "In bed."

"*Sí*, and that is where a man and woman are most vulnerable." He crossed his arms over his chest to keep from tossing her over his shoulder, marching into their bedroom, and showing her exactly how good this was between them.

"We never talk."

"We are talking now."

Her eyes narrowed and a disgruntled sigh seethed through the row of perfectly shaped teeth. "We are dancing around the heart of the issue as if we're afraid it will incinerate us."

He paced to the patio door and stared out at the night, annoyed she'd tossed his fears back in his face. He did hate to place any store in emotions, for they weakened him. They stripped him of control.

Right now he didn't dare lose the upper hand again. He turned and crossed back to her, his blood heating as her eyes flared with the desire she couldn't deny.

"From the first moment I saw you, I wanted you," he said, that admission coming easy.

"For sex," she interrupted.

"*Sí.* But you surprised me even in that," he said, and held up a hand when she made to toss in her opinion again. "I had never felt that heart-stopping attraction to another woman. Never!"

The icy sheen in her eyes melted, revealing a vulnerability that had him aching to draw her close to his heart. "It was different for me, too. I'd never felt so drawn to a man before."

"Then we are in agreement," he said.

"Not entirely," she said, a whisper of unease tickled his nape when she moved closer and laid her small hand over his pounding heart. "If our desire for each other waned—"

"It won't," he interrupted, sensing where she was going with this and dreading what was to come if he didn't divert her.

"What would we have to bind us together?" she asked anyway.

¡Hostias! He wasn't about to answer that question for the obvious reason would only take the edge off the hurt they'd caused each other without solving a thing.

"A family if we are so fortunate," he said and the intense longing in her eyes brought a thick lump of emotion to his throat.

Her hand dropped from his chest, and he was finally able to draw a decent breath. "And if we're not so fortunate?"

He swiped a hand over his face and quashed the tremor rippling through him. He'd rather square off against angry board members amid a hostile takeover than guess what the future held for him and Allegra.

"We could adopt," he said.

She looked away as if she couldn't stand the sight of him. "You're still using a child to keep us together. I need more than that from you."

It was his turn to seethe, for he feared he'd never understand the mind of a woman. Especially this small, fierce one standing before him who challenged him to bare his soul.

She turned to walk away. He grabbed her arm and yanked her back to him and she slammed into his chest with a startled squeal.

"I'll give you everything you desire in due time." And before she could protest or launch into another argument, his mouth captured hers at the same time.

The instant his lips touched her soft trembling ones, he tucked her against him and settled in for a long, slow assault on her senses. They were meant to be together for all time. Why couldn't she see it? Why couldn't she be content to know that he'd give anything to make her happy?

Her soft moan hummed through his senses, the flint that set his blood on fire as her lips molded to his in a perfection he'd never felt with another. This was his woman. She'd been his from the moment he'd set eyes on her on a Cancún beach. She'd always be his. His!

Her hands clutched at his shirt, clinging to him in a sultry capitulation that stroked his pride. That tremor of surrender that shot through her shook his body with the force of an earthquake.

She was sweet seduction and spicy desire, and he was ravenous to feast on their passion. With her, his control was a tenuous thing. But he wouldn't take her right now on the heels of an argument.

No, that would only reinforce her assumption that he only wanted her for sex. He wasn't about to pick that thread again, for if he wasn't careful his whole world would ravel on him again.

Control. It was all about control and his refusal to relinquish it, even in this.

He set her from him, hating that his heart continued to drum with need. He had to wait a tense moment before he trusted himself to speak.

"Is something wrong?" she asked, her eyes slow to focus, too, after that scorching kiss.

"It has been a long day." He trailed two fingers over her cheek and smiled when she trembled. "After we eat supper, I will give you a tour of the *casa*."

Allegra wanted to scream in frustration as Miguel banked the desire that was still raging in her. How could he set her aside after such a blisteringly hot kiss? How could he profess to want her, yet throw up an insurmountable wall at the same time?

His spicy scent filled her senses and commanded her full attention, much like he did when he walked into a room. Or when he looked into her eyes with a sensual heat that was so intense her resolve to stay angry at him melted away.

It was so easy to get drunk with love for this man. And so hard to understand what made him tick.

She set out the plate of meats and cheese while he uncorked a bottle of wine. This time the silence between them pulsed with warmth, and she found it impossible to hold her annoyance with this arrogant man who'd stolen her heart.

"I've often thought that I should have refused to marry you," she said as they sat down to eat, and for once meant it.

He snorted and filled his plate, his back so stiff she was certain steel coated his spine. "Your condition left you with no other choice, for I'd not father a bastard."

"You surely don't believe you could have forced me to marry you?" she asked.

"Do you doubt I could?"

She wouldn't dignify that with a reply that would only feed his ego.

He smiled, though it was more a flash of teeth. "I don't recall you resisting my proposal, *querida*."

"That's because I was over the top for you."

He tipped his head back and studied her, and she wondered again what went through his hard head. Did he love her? Or was she simply another possession?

The intensity of his gaze made her flush from head to toe, for there was no mistaking what he wanted from her most. A sex partner at his beck and call.

She wanted more. She wanted purpose in her life.

"I'd like to establish a school for the Mayan children," she said.

Dark eyes honed in on hers with rapt interest. "You are serious?"

"Yes. I need something worthy to do, and since you won't allow me to be a part of your world," she said, emphasizing the last word. "I'll create my own."

"All right. Tell me what you require and I'll hire staff and see that it's done."

"No. I want to do this, Miguel."

His eyebrows slammed together in an angry vee. "There is no need for my wife to work."

She pressed her palms on the table and matched his glower across the table. "Yes, there is. I want to establish a school in Cristobel's name, and I want to take an active part in it."

"Fine, draw up your plans and outline your curriculum," he said. "But I won't allow you to trek into the jungle every day to work."

He infuriated her. She had no freedom with him. She had to make him see that she was an individual, a person with needs. The closure she returned to find eluded her, for her memory was still vague. And she was still caught under Miguel's rule.

She glanced at the *sala* and saw an artfully restored room that was warm and relaxed. It was designed for children to run and play in. It reflected her likes and tastes everywhere, right down to the framed photos of her and his baby that graced the long heavy mantel.

There was a cozy quality to the *sala* that drew her attention. It was a beautiful home that reflected good taste and fine appointment. She appreciated the fact that it was set far from the bustle of the cities, and removed from his family.

But a house wasn't a home until two people put their hearts and souls into it. They'd not established that at Hacienda Primaro because that was and always would be his mother's home.

They didn't have it here because there was nothing of them in this house but a few photographs. There was nothing within to reflect a deep abiding love that would sustain them through the troubled times because the love found here was one-sided.

That was part of the reason why their marriage failed

before when tragedy struck. She wasn't sure they could withstand another cruel blow.

She loved Miguel. She'd always love him. But could she live with a man who kept her apart from his life? A man who treated her like a possession instead of his life partner?

This was not how Miguel envisioned this homecoming to be. Part of her gloom stemmed from the fact he'd extracted a promise from her to stay. Ok, so he'd blackmailed her.

He had to do something to get her to stay. Now that she was here, she'd thrown up another wall for him to scale. This one called to his heart, for what better tribute could he have for his *niña* than to establish a school in her name?

"Are you brooding because it's too dangerous for you to teach?" he asked, jarring her from her dark musings.

She shook her head. "No, I'm just wondering what the future holds if we stay married."

He should have guessed she was back to that again.

"Was it that bad being my wife?" he asked, determined to try a different tactic and find out what drove her from him.

She frowned, drawing in on herself again, ruminative, making him sweat out her reply. "Not in the beginning. But before Cristobel was born, you left me."

He made an expansive gesture to include the house. "This was the main reason why I was absent then."

Her gaze met his, and he cringed at the hurt shadowing hers. "To build this. But I didn't know that. You just left our bed without any explanation. You stayed away for a month."

¡Dios mio! It had not been by choice. "I told you I did so out of concern for your condition."

She shook her head, as if finding his excuse unbelievable. "You didn't have to go away because we had to refrain from making love. But I suppose that's all we really had to hold us. The day we were advised to abstain you moved out," she said, her chin lifted in a show of defiance she used to hide hurt feelings. "And after Cristobel was born, you visited me in the hospital, but you didn't come home."

He slid both arms around her and fit her against him, letting her feel his need, desperate to run his hands over her creamy skin that felt like velvet, drink in her unique scent of heady flowers and innocence.

"The doctor warned me to refrain from making love with you before the birth, and afterward, *querida*. I feared I would reach for you in the night and you would welcome me into your arms, so I stayed away from the temptation."

She laughed without humor. "You don't fear anything, Miguel."

Sí, he did. He was terrified of the emotions she ignited in him, for no woman had ever commanded so much of his waking and sleeping thoughts. His libido overrode his good judgment where she was concerned. In all honesty he was scared of loving her as he ached to do.

"Besides," she said with a telling quaver in her voice, "I would have stopped you from going too far."

"Are you sure, *querida?*"

His gaze slid up her in a slow lick of fire. Her eyes widened and a sexy flush kissed her cheeks. She shook her head and backed up, each step slow and hesitant.

He smiled and advanced on her step for step, determined to take great pleasure proving she was as incapable as he at stopping this wildfire that burned between them.

CHAPTER ELEVEN

WITHOUT a doubt Miguel oozed masculine prowess and feline grace. She could picture him as a Spanish conquistador laying siege to this primal land. Or a matador standing proud and unafraid before a snorting, pawing bull. Or the dashing bandito who'd captured her on the beach that long ago day and stole her heart.

"Sex isn't the answer for everything," she said, wildly desperate to temper her desire that was spiraling out of control for she wanted to take this slow and savor every second.

The passion burning in Miguel's dark, mesmerizing eyes melted a river of need within her. Just one look and she was wet and ready for him. One touch and her body would combust from pent-up need.

He bent his head and dropped a trail of kisses down her neck and the scrape of his whiskers sent shivers whispering over her skin. "It is most of the time where we are concerned."

She closed her eyes on a moan of surrender, hating that she capitulated so easily to him and loving that he gave her no option. Oh, God, yes, this was a fabulous idea, for when they made love they did so with abandon. And why in the world was she fighting this need anyway?

Though she'd nearly convinced herself that having sex with

Miguel would make her leaving him more painful, she couldn't stop the desire that pounded in her veins. She'd deal with the self-recriminations and heartache if and when the time came.

He'd dominated her thoughts and desires for six long lonely months. That tumble they'd had in the bathhouse was just that—a wickedly delicious tumble. She wanted more— she wanted all he had to give her.

She cupped his jaw and brought his face to her. Their mouths collided in a fury of raw need, feeding on each other until she gasped for breath. This was heaven, she thought.

She'd indulge in all he had to offer in this house he'd built for them. Perhaps then they could deal with the lies and loss that drove them apart.

He yanked her shirt off and flicked open her bra with one slick move, releasing breasts that swelled and strained for his touch. She arched against him as his strong hands claimed her bosom, cupping and kneading them until she thought she'd die from the pleasure, flicking and rolling her taut nipples until she begged him to take them into his mouth. How had she lived without this?

"We will go slow next time, *carino*," he said as his hot mouth finally closed over one hard, throbbing peak.

He sucked hard on one engorged tip, and a bolt of heat shot through her to pierce the dam of desire she'd held back for so long. She threaded her fingers through his thick hair that felt like raw silk and surrendered to the sensations rocketing through her.

"Yes," she whispered as she dropped her head back and released the moan trapped in her.

The love she'd felt for him was there, a bit bruised but still strong. Still hopeful.

Dare she risk all with this man again?

He'd never included her in his world. He'd never shared

his plans. He was demanding and arrogant and the sexiest man she'd ever met.

But he wanted her back, and how could she walk away? How could she give up on them now, after they'd lost so much?

They couldn't. It was laughable now to think they could indulge in farewell sex and walk away. For when they were locked in the throes of passion, nothing else mattered.

Not revenge.

Not regrets.

Not the shroud over her memory.

For now all that mattered was the sensations exploding within her. Her hands swept down his back, thrilling as his muscles bunched and rippled beneath her touch. She hated the barrier of clothes that robbed her of glorying in the touch and taste of his warm, bare flesh.

She grabbed handfuls of the jersey that molded over his powerful torso and yanked hard. The cloth ripped at the seams, and the sound heightened her arousal and dredged a sensuous moan from her.

He raised his arms to oblige her, his mouth hitching in the barest smile that had her stopping just to admire his masculine beauty. His eyes were dark and drowsy with passion and she quaked so badly she nearly came then.

"Impatient, *querida*?"

"You know I am."

She'd waited a lifetime for the steely length of her husband to fill her again, for his hands to stroke her to climax. And to prove it, she slipped her arms around his waist and ran her tongue from the upper ridge of his hard abs to one beaded male nipple.

He tossed his head back and growled his pleasure. She felt his impressive length throb against her stomach as he walked her backward, his fingers tangled in her hair.

He dropped on the sofa and dragged her down atop him. This was how she wanted him!

She straddled his hot, hard length and continued her assault. He mumbled something in Mayan and captured her mouth in a deep drugging kiss that narrowed her world to this man, this moment.

Her fingers fumbled with his zipper, her mind so dulled by passion she finally gave up and rubbed his impressive arousal through his jeans.

"Clothes," she said when they finally came up for air, her tone a complaint that loosed an annoyed laugh from him.

He set her on her feet, then stood as well and rid himself of his jeans with an economy of movement.

It was all she could do to stand as she admired this man of her heart. He was heavy with desire for her, and knowing she'd brought him to this state sucked the moisture from her mouth and weakened her knees.

He was as lean and well muscled as a jaguar. She knew now he'd honed that gorgeous body with hard work in the villages.

She reached out to touch him.

He drew her close, but instead of kissing her again he swept her off her feet and strode to the bedroom. The whole way she nibbled at the strong column of his throat and the proud jut of his chin until she felt the tremors in his strong arms.

"You will be treated in kind," he said in a voice rasping with passion.

"I'm counting on it."

He dropped her on the bed and followed her down, covering her in one long, lean stretch that set her senses on fire. God how she'd missed this man, this feeling of oneness.

She inhaled his spicy scent, her legs parting instantly to accommodate him, her hands glorying as they swept up his strong back to latch onto his powerful shoulders.

The kiss was far too brief. He heaved off her and she made a moue of protest.

"Clothes," he said, and made short work of removing her jeans.

He hooked his thumbs under the lacy edge of her knickers and she lifted her hips so he could rip them off as well. But he seemed in no hurry while her body was screaming for him to come back to her and ease this ache.

He stopped, his eyes widening marginally. She knew he'd seen the scar right above the hairline, the mark of a hasty surgery that had done more damage than good.

She wanted to hide from the awful truth, feeling ugly inside. But then he bent to press kisses along the scar and her heart nearly stopped. Tears stung her eyes, but the heat of passion soon dried them.

He lifted his head, his eyes ablaze with desire and compassion so strong her breath caught. His thumbs grazed her mons in one slow, possessive caress before sliding over the damp folds of her sex to make her squirm and reducing her world to this moment. He teased her with one finger, and a jolt of heat rocketed through her to bring her hips bucking off the bed.

"Have you forgotten how?" she asked when he continued to touch her until she was ready to scream from want.

"Are you insinuating I'm taking too slow?" he asked, his voice thick and his accent more pronounced as he dragged the knickers down her legs in slow, tantalizing seconds, the pads of his fingers skimming her flesh until she trembled so deeply she shook the bed.

"Yes!" To prove it, she wrapped her fingers around his sex.

She didn't want slow or easy, but fast and hard. She wanted him inside her. Now. Filling her. She didn't want him staring at her, concerned he might hurt her, for the waiting was painful enough.

He managed to hike one eyebrow, but he did as she bid.

"Now," she said, spreading her legs wider to accommodate him.

"Not yet."

He shifted his body and ran his tongue up her thigh. She bucked and felt her own dampness. Her sex throbbed, her breasts tightened into aching mounds.

Her breath escaped her in short, restive pants until she thought she'd die. His first intimate kiss was so deep and so commanding she came in a heartbeat.

Too fast, too fast. But she couldn't form the words as he covered her body with his.

His gaze searched hers, the carnal need in his making them black. His sex probed her opening once before pushing into her in one swift, conquering thrust. She gasped at the exquisite power pulsing within her and locked her legs around his waist, her fingers digging into his corded arms.

This was what she'd mourned, too, far longer than anything else. She bowed into him and buried her face in his neck, aroused by his musk that drugged her senses, reveling in the salty tang of his skin.

For a heartbeat they stayed like that, joined in body, but not moving, not breathing. She let her body say what her pride refused to let her voice, words that would separate them again and deprive her of this closeness.

If she could just contain her emotions when passion overtook her again, but she couldn't control herself around him. That much had never changed.

His long, strong fingers skimmed down her sides to cup her bum, lifting her. *"Mi amanate, mi esposa,"* he whispered roughly, his expression as fiercely possessive as his hold on her.

Like the night of their wedding, his vow was the same. Hearing it again after so long brought tears to her eyes, for though she was both his lover and wife this night, it wouldn't last. It couldn't, for there was too much pain between them to go back to those days. But if they could…

He rocked his lean hips, thrusting into her in another deep, long stroke that thrummed her heart and numbed her mind. The pain and emptiness that had been her companion for so long vanished, replaced by a sense of oneness that defied the odds facing them.

His mouth closed over hers, his tongue awakening a host of new sensations. That he could make love to her mouth with the same finite care as his sex did to hers splintered her control.

Her hands feathered down his sides and held on tight as the pressure built inside her until she feared she'd explode. Still he adored her with hands and mouth and sex until she splintered in his arms, screaming his name.

Her own name echoed around her, his voice deep and husky as he rocked into her one last time and stiffened. She clung to him, her body quivering inside and out as ripples of pleasure rocked through her, carrying her along the aftershocks of his own explosive climax.

It ended too soon. She lay there, unwilling to be the first to move and break the spell. For this closeness was glorious and freeing and she wanted far more.

She wanted to make love with him again.

She wanted forever with him.

He shifted, his weight lifting off her, his hair-roughened legs teasing skin sensitized by his touch, his possession. She soaked up the sensations, desperate to brand new memories on her mind, ones that would last her an eternity.

"Now we will go slow," he said, and matched action to words by capturing her mouth in one long, languorous kiss that sang through her blood, stealing any protest she'd dare make, tempting her to give herself over to him again.

"You seem arrogantly sure of yourself," she murmured against the full curve of his lips when the kiss finally broke and they'd both dragged in air.

He dropped a line of wet, hot kisses down her throat, pausing at the pulse point. For one moment she felt his heart beating in tandem with hers.

"Do you doubt my prowess?" His mouth opened on her right breast, his tongue swirling the taut nipple into an aching peak.

"Never."

She arched against him, her fingers sliding through the silk of his hair to grip his head and hold him tight. Her hips lifted as well in invitation to the hard length of his sex pulsing against her belly.

He shifted, cupping her face in his big hands, his eyes twin embers of coal that burned so hot she felt the heat sear her soul. "You are mine, *querida*."

But for how long?

She ran a shaky finger along the strong line of his jaw, skimming chiseled lips that filled her with love with one rare smile, brought her to ecstasy with kisses that muddled her mind, or broke her heart with one damning scowl.

She made to pull away, but his mouth swooped down on hers, stilling her protest. She wanted to resist him, but she couldn't. Wanted to hate him for controlling her body with a look, a touch, a kiss. Wanted to find closure and end her own inner torment, but she knew that would never happen until her memory finally returned.

The pleasure was too great in his arms, and she was helpless to resist him.

Miguel sprawled on his back in bed, an arm thrown over his eyes. Allegra snuggled beside him, having surrendered to exhaustion hours ago.

But sleep eluded him.

Before her return, he'd convinced himself that he could romance her, steal her heart again, tease her with dreams of starting over and then desert her as she'd done him. He was prepared to lull her into a false complacency if he must as a means to his end. He'd wanted her to hurt as she'd hurt him.

But he hadn't known both their families had schemed to keep them apart. How uncanny he'd been out of the country on a mercy mission for his people at the time of the accident.

He'd had no idea of the tragedy awaiting him at home. While he was risking his life with the *Médecins sans Frontiéres* to help the *campesinado* in the hinterlands of Guatemala, his family was being ripped apart.

It was no wonder that Loring whisked Allegra back to England when three weeks passed and Miguel had failed to make any contact with his desperately ill wife. He suspected if the truth be known, his own *madre* had suggested it.

For she'd have decreed Allegra more of an unfit wife than she had before they'd married. She'd have expected him to produce another heir, and that probability was dismal with Allegra.

He pinched the bridge of his nose, disgusted with himself for believing the lies and half-truths. Most of all, he hated that he'd failed her.

The sleeping woman at his side stirred, releasing a moan that was soft as a whisper yet raised the hairs on his arms. Did her subconscious replay the accident?

Miguel reached out to brush back the strands of hair from her pale face. Her cheeks were wet and hot from the silent tears she held back when she was awake.

His chest felt too tight to draw a decent breath. He'd been ill-prepared when he'd come here, for he'd done so in the heat of anger to prove to Allegra that their future had been foremost on his mind.

Now that she'd seen it, now that he had her promise she was staying with him, it was time to move in fully.

But, he still had an obstacle to clear up. Before the day was out, he'd know why his *madre* lied to him. He wanted her to look him in the eye and tell him why she'd set out to destroy his marriage.

He rose from the bed and strode into the *sala*. Now that he'd set his mind on a course of action, he wanted this over with. He rolled his shoulders against the impatience that worked his muscles into knots.

He stood there a moment as the first glimmer of morning brushed orange swaths across a pink horizon. The blush of dawn inched through the windows and across the tile floors, bringing the terra cotta to life.

The day would be bright without clouds to shadow the truth.

"You're up early," she said.

He turned to find her standing in the bedroom doorway, the sheet gathered round her for modesty's sake. Her hair was mussed—sexy.

Her chest rose and fell too fast. Her gaze left a burning trail from his chest to his groin.

Her mouth parted slightly as her tongue darted out to wet her sensuous lips. This was the look of carnal hunger that he remembered well of her.

Lust bolted through him. His blood heated and raced. His sex sprang awake and thickened.

He didn't attempt to hide his evident desire for her. "We need to return to Hacienda Primaro soon."

"I—I'd like to shower first."

He smiled and started toward her. "Then we shall do so together to save time."

One delicate eyebrow lifted in question, a knowing smile teasing the lips he longed to ravish. "It never did before."

He paused before her to loosen her grip on the sheet. "Are you complaining?"

"No."

The sheet slithered down her body, unveiling her curves like a curator would a prize statue. Though her skin was the delicate hue of fine porcelain, she was a warm, willing woman.

His woman.

But the emotion in her eyes before she lowered her gaze turned his throat dry.

It was adoration.

The same emotion he'd seen on her face countless times when she'd professed her love for him.

He'd been arrogantly amused by it when their relationship was young and full of promise. He'd never expected his own heart to swell with love for her, or break when he learned she'd been unfaithful. He had been determined to reject love for that very reason, and now he knew the pain of loss.

He'd never given that much of himself to another before—he'd never lost control of his emotions except with her.

Sí, he'd closed himself off from it before. But he couldn't do that now. No, he'd have to deal with it this time.

CHAPTER TWELVE

IT WAS early evening by the time Miguel and Allegra arrived at the Hacienda Primaro. He'd made several phone calls as he drove, speaking in Spanish so rapidly she caught very little of the conversation other than mention of Riveras in a tone so vehement she shivered.

Whatever Miguel decided to do with the man couldn't be punishment enough. Admitting that made her wonder if she'd become as ruthless as her husband, or if this was the closure she'd desperately sought and found.

"Tell Señora Barrosa I wish to speak with her now," Miguel said to the housekeeper as soon as they walked in the door.

"She isn't here, *señor*." The housekeeper explained that Miguel's mother had gone on a shopping jaunt to Merida with her daughter and wasn't expected back until tomorrow. "Would you and the *señora* wish for something to eat?"

"Nothing for me, thank you," Allegra said.

Miguel ordered a sandwich, and insisted Allegra at least have a plate of fruit and cheese to nibble on. Food didn't appeal in the least, but she didn't argue.

"If you don't mind," she said. "I'd like to rest."

His eyes glowed a rich mocha that warmed her within. "By

all means rest. You did not get much sleep last night, and tonight will be the same."

She couldn't stop the fiery blush from blazing over her face, no more than she could stay the languid desire that swirled within her. She gave his impressive physique an appreciative once-over and was rewarded with a deep, masculine groan of longing.

"Perhaps you should take a nap as well."

He laughed, a liquid rumble that sounded free and wicked, like the man she'd first met on the beach what seemed a lifetime ago. "If we retired to our rooms to take a nap now," he said, his expression conveying that he'd like nothing better, "I can promise you that we would not rest."

She was more than aware of that, too. She actually wanted to lose herself in his arms, for then she didn't have to face the uncertainty in her life.

She didn't have to wonder how long it would be before the flames of their desire would die out. She wouldn't have to deal with the pain of knowing one day he'd turn to another woman who'd give him children.

"Great sex never solved any of our problems, or even began to mend the differences that pulled us apart," she said.

He cocked one dark eyebrow. "Are you weary of our arrangement so soon?"

"I'm just tired," she said. "I'll be in my room."

"Our room," Miguel said, looking more like a fierce Mayan warrior than a billionaire in soft faded denims and a black T-shirt that molded over his muscular chest. "I will join you in an hour, *querida*."

He turned and strode off the opposite direction toward his office. He'd likely be there for an hour or more.

Her body quivering at the sultry promise in his voice she struck off down the hall toward the sleeping quarters. Her heels clicked a discordant beat on the tiles that mirrored her soul. Though Señora Barrosa wasn't in residence, the *casa* felt cold and sterile. Try as she might, she'd never been able to imagine Miguel and his sister playing in this house, running down the halls, their laughter ringing off the warm plaster walls.

It was a showpiece. A *casa* built to impress. Even the altars devoted to the deceased family members lacked anything personal.

She paused at the small alcove that housed the altar devoted to Cristobel. Her heart swelled with love as she smiled at the framed photo of her beautiful newborn baby.

A tiny rosary hung from a corner of the frame with a pacifier and rattle lying on the lace cloth. She reached over and ran her fingers over the fleece ear of the stuffed bear she'd bought for Cristobel.

Unlike the exquisite porcelain doll reposed on the other side, her child could have played with the stuffed toy. She could have been a child without a care.

Despite the fact she felt the pull of her mother-in-law even here, this tradition gave her such a sense of peace that she decided she'd create a similar one in the new *casa*. Even if she didn't live there for long, perhaps it would offer Miguel peace. Perhaps he'd pause from his rat race of making more millions and share a quiet moment with the memory of his daughter.

With her spirits lifted a bit, she moved on to the master suite and crawled up on the big bed. She hadn't slept in this room with Miguel since she was eight months pregnant.

Her cheeks warmed, for she doubted she'd get much sleep tonight. But for now she'd rest.

The slamming of a door deep in the house woke her. She stretched, feeling more rested than she had in days. And why shouldn't she?

A glance at the bedside clock proved she'd slept several

dreamless hours. She frowned. Why hadn't Miguel joined her as promised?

She slid from the bed and went stone-still as the memory of Amando Riveras blazed across her mind. My God! She could see it clearly. She saw what he'd done. She had to tell Miguel.

Allegra left the bedroom and set off toward his office, suspecting he'd gotten involved in managing his empire and completely forgot about the woman in his bed. She burst into the room with a chiding retort poised on her lips, only to find the room empty.

"Miguel?"

No answer other than the soft hum of his computer. She wandered the room and paused to scan the bookshelves, but as the minutes ticked past and he didn't return, her restlessness grew.

She rounded his desk with the intention of finding a pen and paper to leave him a note, giving the screen no more than a passing glance. The name bolded on the subject line of an e-mail made her blood run cold.

Why would her uncle Loring be the subject of communication?

She dropped onto his chair and read the e-mail, her stomach knotting as the meaning sank in. It was from Miguel's attorney and it detailed everything that Loring Vandohrn owned, from his meager savings to the quaint cottage he lived in.

His comings and going were noted as well, confirming Miguel had had him watched closely. Recently, too, judging by the dates.

The scuff of a shoe brought her gaze snapping up to his. The strong line of his jaw looked harder than granite, and his eyes were just as dark and emotionless.

"You liar!" She bolted to her feet, so angry she shook. "You promised you wouldn't ruin my uncle."

"I haven't."

"But you plan to," she said, sick inside that he'd promise her one thing yet do another.

He strode toward her in no particular hurry. "That is insurance, *querida*. I won't use it unless I must."

"And of course I am to blindly believe you," she said.

"*Sí*, for it is the truth."

Truth and lies. There were so many between them.

"Is there a reason, besides eavesdropping, that you are reading my e-mail?" he asked as he rounded the desk.

She skittered backward to put distance between them. "I came here to tell you I'd remembered Riveras's involvement with the refugees. When you weren't here, I thought to leave you a note."

He lifted one brow and reached over to click off the screen. "Please, go on."

"It was when I overheard Riveras demanding money from them, that I knew I had to get away from him."

"Was he aware that you knew of his operation?" he asked.

"Yes. I was afraid," she said, and felt a chill tiptoe over her as the memory cleared. "I had to get away, but I hadn't a clue of your whereabouts, so I went straightway to your mother."

He shrugged, but his fisted hands belied his rage. "She didn't know."

"Señora Barrosa was her usual caustic self and refused to tell me where you'd gone until I told her I was leaving." She made a face at that unpleasant memory, for their argument was insulting and mean. "She told me you were in Cancún on business."

"*¡Dios mio!* I was out of the country."

"I didn't know that then. I wanted to find you because I was afraid to stay here with Riveras," she said. "So I packed what I needed, bundled Cristobel up and prepared to leave before he could return and stop me."

"My *madre* told me much the same story, though she didn't admit she'd told you I was in Cancún," he said, then scowled. "She added that she saw you taking the jewelry from the safe."

"That's a lie! I didn't take it."

"And yet it disappeared when you did."

Her gaze fixed on his unreadable one. "You think I stole them."

"It was a reasonable assumption."

That hurt. "You wouldn't say that if you truly knew me," she said, and had the satisfaction of seeing a ruddy tinge darken the sculpted curve of his cheekbones.

"But that is the point," he said. "We know each other in bed, but not so much out of it."

It was a truth she couldn't deny. They'd made love every chance they got, and they'd made a baby. Yet they had been isolated from on another in marriage.

"Where were you?" she asked, not sure if he'd even answer her.

He scrubbed a hand over his nape. "Guatemala. I went on a mercy mission in the jungle."

She gripped the back of the nearest chair and leaned into it. "You could have been killed."

"*Sí,* but I wasn't," he said. "But that's why I had no idea what had happened until I returned home nearly three weeks after the accident."

Allegra rubbed her forehead as reality rose like a Mayan temple above the sultry mists of the rain forest. Miguel hadn't been off in Cancún on business or pleasure.

He'd been deep in the Guatemalan jungle helping the displaced Mayans. That singular humanitarian effort he kept hidden from the world endeared him more to her, for it showed a depth of spirit and compassion he kept hidden.

"Why didn't you tell me about your mission work among the Mayan?" she asked.

He shrugged, his shoulders stiff, his back an unyielding straight line. "It is not my habit to divulge my plans to anyone, especially when secrecy of a mission is paramount."

"I wasn't anyone, Miguel. I am your wife," she said.

"What difference would it have made if you'd known?" he asked, the cynical curl to his lip firmly in place, his dark eyes shuttered as well.

"I wouldn't have gone to the beach house," she said.

For she was sure Amando Riveras would have caught her there and silenced her for good.

Miguel paced the room, swore and barely—barely—quelled the urge to drive his fist into something. It was far preferable to strangling his wife for the propensity to walk headlong into danger.

His chest heaved with the anger building in him now, for he'd charged a man to do the job she took on without hesitation, a task she completed alone and expertly. Just thinking of the danger she placed herself in terrified him.

He hated feeling that emotion for one second!

"You are reckless to a fault," he said.

"I am not."

"*Sí*, you are," he said. "You risked your life by getting involved with the refugees. You left here twice without thought to the danger you were in."

She jammed her hands at her sides and glared at him. "I had good reasons."

He snorted and crossed his arms over his chest. "That is a

matter of opinion. And since it is my opinion that decided the rules here," he said, "you will not leave here alone again."

"I will not live in a prison." With that, she whirled and stomped from his office.

Tears of anger stung the backs of her eyes, but she blinked them away. She'd come for closure. Well, this was as close as it would get.

She paused at the altar, taking a last longing look at her daughter. The small stuffed bear she'd bought for Cristobel called out to her.

Without hesitating, she gathered it close just as Miguel stormed up to her. "What are you doing?"

"Taking the bear I bought for my daughter," she said.

"Why?"

"Because I want it," she said. "I've decided to build an altar for her in my home."

He plucked the porcelain doll off the altar and handed it to her. "Then take this, too."

She shook her head and backed away. "The doll isn't mine."

"Take it anyway," he said, challenge blazing in his eyes. "Cristobel would've liked it."

She wasn't sure what surprised her most. That he was not balking about her taking the bear, or that he believed their daughter would have liked the doll.

"The bear is enough."

"Take it." He made to stuff the doll under her arm.

She jerked back at the same time. The doll dropped to the terra cotta tiles and shattered, the sound loud.

"Now look what you've done!" She glanced from the broken doll and its too blue glass eye to Miguel.

"What I have—"

He broke off, his dark gaze riveted on the heap of shattered porcelain. He squatted beside it and picked up the glistening eye.

"*¡Maldita sea!* This is a blue topaz." Before what he said registered, he'd upended what remained of the doll and shook it.

Glittering jewels poured onto the floor in a rainbow spray of color.

She blinked, unable to believe her eyes. "Is that the jewelry I was accused of stealing?"

"*Sí.*" His fury was so great he could barely hold a coherent thought. His *madre* had done this.

There could be no other explanation.

There could be no greater deceit.

She'd hidden the jewelry in the doll, and let him believe Allegra had stolen them. She'd let his hatred fester for his wife. How many other lies had she spewed to cause him grief?

No wonder she was unnerved when he brought Allegra back to the *casa*.

"Why does she hate me so much?" Allegra asked as she squatted beside him.

He gathered up the jewelry, still baffled by the workings of his *madre*'s mind. "Because she is a bitter woman."

"What are you going to do?"

What he should have done when he brought his bride home the first time. "I will deal with *madre* in due time."

"I'm sorry she's done this to us."

So was he, for this cruel act was beyond forgiveness.

"Where are you going?" he asked when he realized she was walking away.

"To the cemetery to visit my daughter's grave."

He shot to his feet, the missing jewelry clenched in his fists. "I forbid you to go out alone again."

That brought her up short. She faced him, her eyes glittering with an array of emotions that scared the hell out of him. "You've no right to order me about!"

¡Dios mio! He drove his fingers through his hair, frus-

trated and angry with himself and the world. He couldn't repeat history with her again. He had to make her see reason.

"You don't know what the kidnappers can do," he said, drawing on memories he'd shoved to the far recesses of his mind. "It is a common joke that kidnapping is a career in Mexico, but though many people are returned harmless, there are those that delight in torturing their victims first."

The color drained from her face. "I'm sure you're right, but I'm not in the habit of having someone shadow my steps."

"You will have to get used to it."

She bristled, and he knew he'd gone about this all wrong. "Perhaps I will," she said at last. "If I stay."

"You will."

"Are you always this sure of yourself?" she asked, a mocking tone tingeing her voice.

"*Sí*, especially in this."

She must have picked up on his anxiety for she slid him a sideways look. "What aren't you telling me, Miguel?"

He tipped his head back and huffed out an annoyed breath, loath to share his darkest hour with anyone.

"Of course, what am I thinking?" Her voice crackled with mockery. "You don't share anything of yourself with me. Forget I asked. Hold your secrets close to your heart and maybe they will keep you warm—"

"When I was eight," he smoothly interrupted her. "I defied my *madre*'s order and took my little brother into the village. It was market day and I knew there would be an array of delights for hungry boys."

"Did you stuff yourselves on sweets?" she asked.

"No. We never made it." He dropped the jewelry on his daughter's altar and crossed to the window, staring out at the hacienda that teemed with more bad memories than good ones. "Two men abducted us just beyond the henequen factory and took us to a remote hut in the jungle. I fought them tooth and nail and escaped, but Diego couldn't break free."

"How awful for you both!" she said and moved close to press a hand to his chest where his heart raced. "They demanded a ransom?"

"Ten thousand dollars a piece." He hated the chill of terror coursing through him that he'd never been able to escape. "My *padre* followed the instructions and gave the money to a servant to deliver. But the money was too great a temptation. He took it and ran. By the time my *padre* realized what he'd done, it was too late."

"What happened, Miguel?"

"The kidnappers hanged my brother in a *palapa* and left him to strangle to death," he said, clenching his jaw as the old pain sliced through him again. "*Padre* found Diego the next day."

Her arms stole around his waist and held on tight while her head found a natural perch against his chest. "Tell me they caught those men."

He rested his chin on the top of her head, breathing in her sweet scent, holding her close to him. "No. They got away, and my *madre* never forgave me for leading my brother into danger."

She sucked in a sharp breath that sizzled with disapproval. "But you were just a child."

He pinched his eyes shut, loath to tell her the rest now, for it made no difference. "I had been repeatedly told of the danger of going off alone." He turned her around so he could look into her eyes that were too big and glistening with unshed tears. "I chose to defy common sense, *querida*. I won't let you do the same because I sure as hell can't go through losing you now that I've found you again."

CHAPTER THIRTEEN

ALLEGRA stared into his dark, troubled eyes, her heart breaking over the tragedy he'd endured as a child. No wonder he was so adamant over her taking a guard along if she left the *casa*.

She'd never dreamed danger lurked so close. Even though he'd warned her to use extreme caution, she'd defied him— not once but for an entire month.

Her solo sojourns came off without a hitch. But the one time she took her daughter away, tragedy struck.

"You should hate me for what I've done," she said, despising herself for being such a fool.

He cupped her face and sent her a depreciating smile that brought a lump of emotion to her throat. "I did hate you, but I hated myself more because I left you in someone else's care instead of being here for you."

"Riveras," she said, and he grumbled in agreement. "There are still parts I can't remember."

"It will come in due time." He skimmed his fingertips over her cheek, the touch so lightly erotic she shivered. "To hell with bad timing and heavy hearts. I want you, *querida.*"

"Sex doesn't fix everything." Even great sex with the person you loved beyond life.

He jammed his hands in his pockets, and for a heartbeat,

she saw the little boy who'd hid his feelings from the world out of duty instead of the extraordinary man who'd marched into her staid world and swept her off her feet. She caught a rare glimpse of the curious child who'd gone on a grand adventure with his little brother and ended up tormented by a cruel tragedy.

"So you're not willing to try?" he asked, his neutral tone the cue that the subject of his brother's kidnapping was closed.

He'd shun empathy on the grounds he didn't deserve any.

He'd ignore any remorse sent his way, for he'd already heaped more on himself than any man should bear.

No, she'd have to couch compassion with passion, for that was the only time he lost any control. Even then she always sensed he held a part of back.

"You know I am," she said.

His sensuous mouth curved in a wry smile that was so masculinely provocative she caught herself smiling back at him. How could she think of anything else now as she stared into his dark, haunted eyes and saw the lonely soul reaching out to her?

"But I won't be just the woman in your bed," she said, her memory of those early days oddly sharper than her recent memory. "I'm serious about having an active role in the school."

She swept her palms over his chest and shivered as her skin tingled with awareness of him as her lover. In turn, her body slowly bloomed at the promise glowing in his eyes.

"That is business." His gaze caressed her with a lover's finesse. "This is pleasure."

"Yes," she whispered, caving in to the sensual stroke of his hands.

If she'd asserted herself before, maybe they wouldn't have drifted apart and this living nightmare wouldn't have happened. Maybe they'd still be a family—Miguel, her and Cristobel.

Maybe they'd have another baby.

That would never happen now. She had nothing to lose but her pride and the chance to love this man with abandon again. She was willing to cast caution aside and stay with him for as long as it lasted this time.

But she'd not take a backseat and be nothing more than his convenient wife. She had to do something useful with her life or she'd not be able to remain here with him.

She shifted, brushing her breasts against the hard wall of his chest in erotic invitation. The contact sent a sensitized charge rocketing through her body to jolt her heart as if fusing them together.

Body tingling with need, she brushed against him again, straddling one thickly muscled leg and pressing against his impressive erection.

It was a blatant taunt for him to take her now. Toss her on the bed, the floor or press her against the wall. Strip her of her constricting clothes and indecisions.

But he merely groaned and stared at her with eyes smoldering with raw passion.

He was making her work for satisfaction. He was giving her time to think this through and change her mind if she wished.

She couldn't draw another breath unless she was in his arms—unless he was inside her, deep and throbbing and filling the empty ache within her.

"We've made far too many mistakes," she said.

"*Sí*, I know." He brushed the full, sensual curve of his lips over hers and the muscles surrounding her sex contracted with a need so intense it took her breath away.

"But I don't regret one moment spent in your arms, Miguel."

"*Carina.*" His mouth captured hers, the kiss deep and drugging, his tongue probing the wet cay of her mouth in a rhythm that made her sex throb and weep for his possession.

"You crave great sex," he said as his mouth left hers to nip along her collarbone.

She craved much more than that. She yearned for his heart. But when he held her, kissed her, caressed her, she ignored the yearnings of her heart to satisfy her libido.

Even now knowing that her nerves hummed with erotic energy, the vibration tightening her nipples before settling between her legs in one long, quivering pulsation. No man had ever affected her so powerfully and masterfully with just a kiss. And when his fingers did slip between her legs and touch her—

She groaned, the sound long and throaty. "Yes, mind-blowing sex with you."

His deep laugh vibrated over her sensitive flesh and sucked her further into the whirlpool of desire. For one wild moment she thought of stopping this madness, then his mouth captured hers in a commanding kiss and the impulse popped like a soap bubble.

He swept her into his arms and headed straight to the bedroom, the thick muscles of his arms and chest tight and clenched and burning hot. That he could carry her was a testimony to his raw strength, for she was sure her legs wouldn't support her.

She threaded her fingers through his thick wealth of hair, anchoring him to her, dizzy drunk with desire. God she loved this man. She'd always love him.

That thought temporarily numbed her as he made short work of ridding them of clothes. She gave a halfhearted effort to shove his T-shirt off, but the tactile feel of his hot skin, bunched muscles and abrasive scrape of black hair beckoned to be explored at leisure.

He pulled her down onto the carpet, his hands boldly stroking her as his mouth claimed hers in a deep kiss that left her breathless and quivering like a just plucked bowstring. Her hands clutched at his broad shoulders as her legs parted to welcome him closer, the movement natural and right.

"Mi amante," he said, the words a sultry caress against her lips as he flexed his lean hips and sank into her pulsing core in one long, deep push.

She bowed her back to pull him in deeper, her nails scoring the taut muscles in his back. "Yes," she said. "God, yes."

For one glorious moment she drank in every nuance of this joining when her body came vibrantly alive. She'd forgotten many things, but she'd never lost a second of making love with Miguel.

Nothing compared to the moment when they came together as lovers, when the world stopped and their hearts beat as one, when they became one. Nothing ever would.

His mouth swooped down on hers, his possession so fierce she trembled. She locked her legs around his lean hips and tried to hold back the explosive need bubbling in her. Tried to control her own emotions. Tried to stretch out this erotically wonderful joining.

But the blood of conquistadors and fierce warriors ran in his veins like a mighty river. Cultured and wild. Ruthless and commanding, never giving an inch.

He knew where she was sensually vulnerable, where to touch her to make her stretch and sigh with pleasure like a sated cat, where to strum and stroke to tighten the thread of desire until she was reduced to a quivering wanton.

She moved with him in this charged erotic dance of lovers, her toes curled on his hair-roughened calves and her blood a deafening roar in her ears. One more thrust, one more intimate stroke, and she came apart in a glittering climax.

She screamed his name and clutched him close, her fingers scoring his back as the spasms went on and on.

He let loose a hoarse shout and rocked into her once more. His long, powerful frame stretched over her, his hands clutching her close, as the aftershock of desire rippled through him again and again, drawing her own climax out with his.

For several, luscious moments they lay there with arms and legs entwined. Bodies joined. Sated. At peace.

On a long sigh that vibrated with male satisfaction, he rested his weight on his elbows and eased from her. "Tomorrow I will deal with my *madre.*"

She stared up into his dark, magnetic eyes and felt her heart seize, for his expression was remote, not giving her a hint of his feelings.

"Do you want me to join you?" she asked, attuned to the muscles tensing in his big, powerful frame that held her prisoner, sensing that he dreaded confronting his mother.

"No. I must do this alone."

Her heart ached that he continued to fight battles alone when she was here to support him any way she could. Could she make him see that it was wrong?

He lowered his head, and she turned her face to avoid the kiss that would surely boggle her mind more. His lips grazed the sensitive skin behind her ear and she shivered and stifled the sigh of pleasure caught in her throat.

"About the school I want to develop," she said, soaking up every delicious second of being cradled in his arms, skin-to-skin, heart to heart.

"No more talking," he said, and captured her mouth with a kiss that was so arrogantly possessive that she could do nothing but sink into him, into desire.

It was enough for now, she thought right before his seductive prowess blotted everything else from her mind but the pleasure she'd found in his arms.

* * *

Quintilla Barrosa was descended from old Castilian stock. Aristocrat with thin ties stretching back to Spain's nobility.

That was clearly evident now as she sat in the *sala* enjoying imported tea. She watched him cross to her with shrewd eyes that were a cold icy-blue.

"Por favor, el verdad," he said and dropped Allegra's jewelry on the side table.

"The truth is ugly."

Not an iota of guilt or remorse registered on her refined face. She wore the mantle of haughty disdain well—a *sangre azul* to her soul.

The wealth of her family lines had vanished, but not the desire to live a life of leisure as was fitting a blue blood. But while Miguel had always known his *madre* held herself superior to even his father, he never dreamed she'd do anything this devious.

"You lied about Allegra's jewels. Why?" Miguel asked, the demand cracking like a whip in the austere room.

Her chin canted to a regal tilt. "I didn't want her to return to claim them, for she wasn't worthy of one piece."

"That was not for you to decide!"

His *madre* cut him a cold, assessing glance. "Even after all she's done, you still want her back. You are a fool."

"She's my wife!"

"A fact that grieves me. While you spent your days and nights ensuring your family would continue to live in comfort, your unfaithful wife was dallying with the guard you hired to protect her!"

A guard who'd nearly brought about her death. A guard who was getting rich off the misfortune of the refugees. "We are talking about your deceit. Not hers."

She huffed in annoyance. "Do yourself a favor and find a woman who can give you children."

"Because you know Allegra can't?"

"What does it matter?"

A great deal. It was the difference between being a protective parent and a vindictively controlling one.

The cold stab of betrayal sank into Miguel's heart at the thought of his *madre* keeping so much from him. "Why didn't you tell me about the details surrounding Allegra's surgery?"

She flung a hand in the air. "If you'd known, you'd have flown off to England and brought her back here."

"*Sí,* you are right."

He tamped down his choking anger and stared at the aristocratic woman before him. She had done an excellent job of painting Allegra in bold, sinister colors. Yet Quintilla Barrosa y Gutierrez wasn't without blame, either, for she'd lied to Miguel when he'd desperately needed the truth.

"I want her out of my *casa,*" his *madre* said.

He inclined his head. "I will take her away tomorrow."

His *madre* visibly relaxed at that. "*Bueno.* When can I expect you to return?"

"I won't," he said, and had the satisfaction of watching the first twinges of unease harden her aristocratic features. "The *casa* is yours to maintain, but the land in mine. I do not have to live here to manage it."

"Where are you going?" she asked.

"My *casa.*"

She sputtered in outrage. "With her?"

Miguel smiled in answer.

"You're making a mistake," she said.

"No, I'm righting a wrong."

"What did she say?" Allegra asked the second Miguel returned to their room. Even her body shimmered with nervous energy while his still pounded with black anger.

"She admitted she'd hid the jewelry in the doll so you couldn't return and claim it," he said. "As for why she lied about your surgery, she decreed you and I should divorce because you are unable to bear children."

She downed her head at that undeniable truth. "So she is guilty of going to extremes to protect her son."

"That was meddling, not protecting," he said. "She will pay for her part in deceiving me."

"You can't be serious," she said. "She's your mother."

His mouth twitched in the parody of a smile. "All my life *madre* was concerned I'd inherently exhibit tendencies of my native lineage."

The remark was lightly delivered, yet she caught an underlying hint of annoyance there. "A waste of energy, for you are certainly the role model for future debonair Hispanic billionaires."

"Then you must thank *Madre,* for if my birth mother would have lived, I would've learned the ways of my Indian ancestors from an early age."

Allegra discounted his observance and honed in on the heart of the issue. "Quintilla isn't your biological mother?"

"No. My *padre* married Quintilla Barrosa when I was barely a year old." He glanced at her, and she read the flicker of pain carved deep in his soul. "My *madre* was Mayan. She died in childbirth."

She digested that news with care, and so much about the man she'd married became clearer. The long weeks he'd spent in the village. The rapport he had with the gentle Mayan Indians. His plans that he'd recently worked on that would bring modern necessities to the remote villages. Water purification systems. Power sources.

His dangerous excursion with the mercy mission into Guatemala.

He wasn't a billionaire looking for a contribution loophole. He was one of the indigenous people, and he hid it from the world. He was helping his people.

The proud Mayan warrior on one hand, and the aristocratic conquistador on the other. She loved both, but she was still far from understanding either side of him.

The trill of his phone rudely interrupted. He answered with a curt, *"¡Hola!"*

Not one emotion showed on his face save the minute tightening of his jaw. He listened for the longest time, and she knew instinctively that the news was bad.

"Por favor, espéreme," he said to the caller and hung up.

"What is it?" she asked.

"There is damage at the beach house. I must leave now."

"You won't shut me out of this, too," she said, more a plea than a demand.

He stared down at her for the longest time, and she saw the war going on inside him this time. He'd never included her in any of his dealings. He'd never even told her what he was involved in, or where he was going.

He was adamantly opposed to her being involved in a school for the Mayans. But she wouldn't back down on that. And she feared he wouldn't, either.

He was having enough difficulty with her insistence of accompanying him to the beach house. Her beach house!

His chest rose and fell, and his lips thinned a fraction. "Very well. We leave for Cancún together."

Allegra grew more apprehensive the closer they got to Cancún. The storm had left its mark across the peninsula, toppling trees and leaving the evidence of flooding in the flattened grass and rivulets carved in the shallow ditches.

Miguel's frown hinted he was surprised by the damage as

well. That only served to increase her worry, for he was a native accustomed to dealing with these storms.

"It is worse than I expected," he said as he turned down the road that led to the beach house.

A small army of people were busy picking up debris strewn everywhere. Though the houses looked intact at first glance, a closer inspection showed the destruction.

He pulled into the last driveway, and Allegra's heart plummeted. The *lamina* roof had been ripped off, and the old mango tree she'd adored had fallen onto the *casa*.

Her spirits sank, for she had wondrous memories of her and Miguel in this house. This had always been the place she came to escape the world.

"Can it be repaired?"

"*Sí, querida,*" he said. "Though it will take time."

Like mending a broken heart?

"I want to see it, Miguel," she said. "I want to know what needs to be fixed."

And she didn't mean just the house but them as well, for she'd been kept in the dark for six long months and she was tired of everyone making decisions for her.

"Okay." His gaze swung back to the beach house and she watched in an odd fascination as his body tensed in increments until he looked carved from stone. "We will inspect the *casa* together. But," he interjected with enough force to freeze her to the sumptuous leather seat, "you will listen to me regarding your safety."

"It's a deal."

They entered through the front door with Miguel leading the way and Allegra following in stunned silence. Her heart sank as she took in the house she'd loved.

The water damage was horrendous, ruining the furnishings and carpets. A strong musty odor hung in the dank air.

She'd met her heart's desire here. She'd returned to find peace. And she'd agreed to his indecent proposal because it gave her one last chance to be with him.

"It will have to be gutted," he said as his leather shoes crunched the grit covering the pasta tiles. "Everything inside is ruined."

"Not everything." She took the small framed photo of Cristobel off the shelf and felt her heart warm.

"How did that survive such destruction?" Miguel asked, coming to stand so close to her she felt his warm breath feather over her nape, felt the heat of him embrace her.

"Divine providence, perhaps," she said, and leaned her back against the strong wall of his chest as she'd done countless times in the early days of their marriage.

His hand skimmed up her bare arm to cup her shoulder, the touch firm and comforting. "I've seen enough here."

She scanned the room and nodded for she knew there was nothing else inside worth saving. It would have to be rebuilt from the ground up. Like their marriage?

Miguel led her outside, but instead of heading toward the car, he guided her toward the beach. Halfway down the incline his hold on her hand changed, his long, blunt fingers entwining with hers and making them one in the public way of lovers.

He stopped at the sea wall at the end of her property and sat, giving a gentle tug for her to join him. She did, their shoulders brushing and hands still entwined.

"So what have you decided," he asked as the cooling breeze whispered off the turquoise sea.

She tipped her face up to the sun and sighed. "About the house?"

He tapped their twined hands on his muscular thigh. "About us?"

"I don't know," she said. "I'm serious about taking an active role in the school."

He heaved a weary sigh and his fingers tightened around hers. "I know that, and I'm serious about keeping you safe."

"You won't stop me then?" She stared into his dark, troubled eyes and saw the war going on within him.

"I won't stop you," he said as he pulled her close and enveloped her in his arms. "We cannot change what is done, but we can start over in our *casa* and build new memories together."

Could they? She was terrified to believe it possible, for there was one thing that neither of them could change. "You'd be happy with a wife and no heir?"

"*Sí,* as long as I have you," he said, and continued that languid glide of his hands up and down her back. "But if you are willing, I'd like you to see a French doctor that I met through the mercy missions. He's a fertility specialist."

She bit her lower lip, knowing that was her only hope. "I'd like that, but there's still no guarantee that I'd conceive."

He skimmed his fingers over her face and her heart stuttered. "We have already learned that there are no guarantees in life. If we can't get pregnant, then there are other options if we really want children."

"Adoption," she said, and he nodded. "I won't go back to the life we had. I won't live my life on the fringe of yours."

"You won't, for you are my equal. My partner." He brushed his lips across hers, the kiss achingly short and sweet. "I won't let you go again."

"That sounds terribly arrogant," she said.

He shrugged. "You are mine, *querida.*"

"And possessive," she said with heat, but she couldn't stop the smile from teasing her mouth.

"You love me." He turned to face her, and the bare emotion

burning in his eyes thawed the cold that had hidden in her for so long. "And I love you. That is why we are going home today."

"You're serious," she asked once she stopped reeling over his avowal of love.

"I would not joke about something as important as us."

He planned to take her home—as in the home he'd built for them. That realization hit her with a tsunami of emotion so strong and pulsing with emotion that she couldn't help but be swept away on it.

"Any objections?" he asked.

"Not one."

EPILOGUE

ALLEGRA CURLED ON a rattan chaise in the shade of the portico and watched her husband.

Despite the odds, Allegra's two surgeries done by the noted French gynecologist had been a huge success. She'd never dreamed she would get pregnant again. How good it was to be wrong!

"You are your father's son," she said as she opened her blouse so two-month-old Diego Estefan Gutierrez could sate his hunger.

How long she'd yearned for a home.

For a child at her breast again.

For the love of her husband.

Her gaze lifted to Miguel's as he reached the portico and squatted beside the chaise, his sensual eyes feasting on her. Her body hummed with awareness as his gaze locked with hers.

"I am jealous," he said and pressed a kiss to her lips that left her blood humming for more.

"You have been neglected the past few months," she said.

"*Sí,* but I'm not complaining."

"Yes, you are," she said without rancor. "But that's all right." She trailed a finger down the center of his chest and warmed at the heat flaring in his eyes. "We'll take care of your needs soon."

One dark eyebrow lifted in mock surprise. "And when would that be, *carino*?"

She sent him a take-me-now smile. "Tonight," she said. "And every one that follows it."

Turn the page for an exclusive extract
from Harlequin Presents®
RAFFAELE: TAMING HIS TEMPESTUOUS VIRGIN
by
Sandra Marton

"In that case," Don Cordiano said, "I give my daughter's hand to my faithful second in command, Antonio Giglio."

At last, the woman's head came up. "No," she whispered. "No," she said again, and the cry grew, gained strength, until she was shrieking it. "No! No! No!"

Rafe stared at her. No wonder she'd sounded familiar. Those wide, violet eyes. The small, straight nose. The sculpted cheekbones, the lush, rosy mouth...

"Wait a minute," Rafe said, "just wait one damned minute...."

Chiara swung toward him. The American knew. Not that it mattered. She was trapped. Trapped! Giglio was an enormous blob of flesh; he had wet-looking red lips and his face was always sweaty. But it was his eyes that made her shudder, and he had taken to watching her with a boldness that was terrifying. She had to do something....

Desperate, she wrenched her hand from her father's.

"I will tell you the truth, Papa. You cannot give me to Giglio. You see—you see, the American and I have already met."

"You're damned right we have," Rafe said furiously. "On the road coming here. Your daughter stepped out of the trees and—"

"I only meant to greet him. As a gesture of—of goodwill."

She swallowed hard. Her eyes met Rafe's and a long-forgotten memory swept through him: being caught in a firefight in some miserable hellhole of a country when a terrified cat, eyes wild with fear, had suddenly, inexplicably run into the middle of it. "But—but he—he took advantage."

Rafe strode toward her. "Try telling your old man what really happened!"

"What *really* happened," she said in a shaky whisper, "is that…is that right there, in his car—right there, Papa, Signor Orsini tried to seduce me!"

Giglio cursed. Don Cordiano roared. Rafe would have said, "You're crazy, all of you," but Chiara Cordiano's dark lashes fluttered and she fainted, straight into his arms.

* * * * *

Be sure to look for
RAFFAELE: TAMING HIS TEMPESTUOUS VIRGIN
by Sandra Marton
available November 2009 from Harlequin Presents®!

Darkly handsome—proud and arrogant
The perfect Sicilian husbands!

RAFFAELE: TAMING HIS TEMPESTUOUS VIRGIN

by

Sandra Marton

The patriarch of a powerful Sicilian dynasty,
Cesare Orsini, has fallen ill, and he wants atonement
before he dies. One by one he sends for his sons—
he has a mission for each to help him clear his
conscience. But the tasks they undertake will
change their lives for ever!

Book #2869

Available November 2009

Pick up the next installment from Sandra Marton

DANTE: CLAIMING HIS SECRET LOVE-CHILD
December 2009

HP12869

HARLEQUIN *Presents*

EXTRA

SNOW, SATIN AND SEDUCTION

Unwrapped by the Billionaire!

It's nearly Christmas and four billionaires are looking
for the perfect gift to unwrap—a virgin perhaps,
or a convenient wife?

One thing's for sure, when the snow is falling outside,
these billionaires will be keeping warm inside,
between their satin sheets.

**Collect all of these wonderful festive titles
in November from the Presents EXTRA line!**

The Millionaire's Christmas Wife #77
by HELEN BROOKS

The Christmas Love-Child #78
by JENNIE LUCAS

Royal Baby, Forbidden Marriage #79
by KATE HEWITT

Bedded at the Billionaire's Convenience #80
by CATHY WILLIAMS

www.eHarlequin.com

HPE1109

REQUEST YOUR FREE BOOKS!

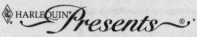 

2 FREE NOVELS PLUS 2 FREE GIFTS!

YES! Please send me 2 FREE Harlequin Presents® novels and my 2 FREE gifts (gifts are worth about $10). After receiving them, if I don't wish to receive any more books, I can return the shipping statement marked "cancel". If I don't cancel, I will receive 6 brand-new novels every month and be billed just $4.05 per book in the U.S. or $4.74 per book in Canada. That's a savings of close to 15% off the cover price! It's quite a bargain! Shipping and handling is just 50¢ per book*. I understand that accepting the 2 free books and gifts places me under no obligation to buy anything. I can always return a shipment and cancel at any time. Even if I never buy another book, the two free books and gifts are mine to keep forever.   106 HDN EYRQ 306 HDN EYR2

Name _____ (PLEASE PRINT)

Address _____ Apt. #

City _____ State/Prov. _____ Zip/Postal Code

Signature (if under 18, a parent or guardian must sign)

Mail to the **Harlequin Reader Service:**
IN U.S.A.: P.O. Box 1867, Buffalo, NY 14240-1867
IN CANADA: P.O. Box 609, Fort Erie, Ontario L2A 5X3

Not valid to current subscribers of Harlequin Presents books.

Are you a current subscriber of Harlequin Presents books and want to receive the larger-print edition? Call 1-800-873-8635 today!

* Terms and prices subject to change without notice. Prices do not include applicable taxes. Sales tax applicable in N.Y. Canadian residents will be charged applicable provincial taxes and GST. Offer not valid in Quebec. This offer is limited to one order per household. All orders subject to approval. Credit or debit balances in a customer's account(s) may be offset by any other outstanding balance owed by or to the customer. Please allow 4 to 6 weeks for delivery. Offer available while quantities last.

Your Privacy: Harlequin Books is committed to protecting your privacy. Our Privacy Policy is available online at www.eHarlequin.com or upon request from the Reader Service. From time to time we make our lists of customers available to reputable third parties who may have a product or service of interest to you. If you would prefer we not share your name and address, please check here. ☐

HP09R

HPI2867